TRANS RITES

AN ANTHOLOGY OF GENDERFUCKED HORROR

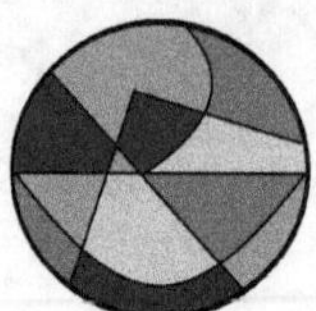 

To Adrian Mellon, who has not been forgotten.

"I wish I could lay in the yard all night
That just feels like home to me
I wish the woods were a viable place to sleep
I keep thinking about my headstone
I keep thinking 'bout what I want it to say
I'm thinking 'bout everything, and I can't get away
I just can't get away."

—Skeleton Drive
"Headstone"

~TABLE OF CONTENTS~

☿

Don't worry, darling.

I see you, and you're safe in my eye; no evil may touch you under my protection, no beast may mark you, no devil deceive you. You are under my watchful gaze, and you are a guest. Heed not the howl in the distance, heed not the rustle in the bushes. You laugh around the campfire with the rest of them, the dirty denim babies and the flannel freaks and the twisted scissor sisters and the fags smoking fags.

I smile at you from across the bonfire, and you smile back, my fingers idly fiddling with the crystal hanging from my neck: honey amethyst, the stone of The Lovers and of Judgement.

You saw the flier on a telephone pole, the ancient wood staple-strewn like a collage of stolen corpses, saw that a local you like was playing at The Winchester Mystery House tonight, saw the grinning face of the Silver Shamrock *jack o'lantern smiling out from black ink scanlined from the cheap library printer that bore it.* Skeleton Drive + Lysistrata Woodrose on Tour! *it proclaimed.* Music at 10—*later than usual for a house show, but considering the time of year, not so unusual.*

Do I look unusual to you, my indigo lips parting and bidding you: come.

The music ended a half hour ago, and it's just stragglers and friends of the house now, sipping ciders and sharing a space bag of Sunset Blush Franzia. *You're not a friend of the house—you're just a face in the crowd, one of the haunted masks. But you stay.*

The girlfriend of the boyfriend of the person who runs the venue passes you a joint, and you put it between your lips, and you breathe up, smoke curling in fractals towards the face of Aiken Drum way up high.

The joint makes the rounds, passing from lung to lung, the lavender mixed with the grass turning the night a menacing purple. I take it between nimble fingers, and you see, unmistakably, when I breathe out, the shape of a circle A.

Commala-come-come, commala-come-one, the smoke beckons. I puff once more and pass, and then I stand and head for the old winnebago parked way back by the blackberry brambles and the brush pile.

You stay there by the fire for a while, expecting to be dismissed by the hosts, but instead they drift back to the house, one by one, until it's just you and the ruler of the roost, the golden-haired thing who books the shows. You wait for them to tell you the night is over, but instead they offer you the last Bell's Two-Hearted from their six-pack and you feel the condensation on the cool glass, slick beneath your fingers.

They smile at you, peering out from behind a pair of pink aviators, and nod towards the camper.

"You taking?" they ask, hitting a nicotine vape and blowing out a caramel apple cloud.

"Taking?" you ask, mouth dry, as if I had breathed that smoky hieroglyph down your throat instead of into the air.

"The afterparty," they say, and begin to head for the house. "If you do decide to just go home, dash the fire, will you? There's a spigot and bucket by the porch."

Instead you watch the flames until they turn into embers, and can almost make out shapes within: a military helicopter spinning into the body of a wolf, a raven-headed woman that becomes a goat-headed man that becomes a dog-faced demon that becomes your own face. The licking tongues twist, twirl, transform—a child bursting into a cloud of botflies, a china doll that breaks and reforms and breaks and reforms, a coin dancing on knuckles.

You blink, and realize that the coin has become solid matter, that it is spinning a white hot dance through the air, and you reflexively reach out to catch it even as it sears the tips of your fingers. As the metal cools, you see an eye on either side, glaring and staring and wide open to swallow the sacrament of the world with hungry white.

It sits on your palm, looking up, and then you follow the thread, hopelessly tangled in it like the Jeremy the crow when he met sweet little Mrs. Brisby-Frisby. Your legs stretch up and you stand there for only a moment before turning and walking towards the string light-strewn awning of my little abode.

Knock, knock, knock, your knuckles against the glass.

You almost turn to run, almost drop the coin and flee, but instead you stand your ground, and then I'm there, haloed in the door.

"Good evening," I smile, sipping my tea and holding it open. "I bid you welcome."

You step into my incensed abode, and see that another mug is already sitting on the table, steaming. As you cross over the threshold, a hairless cat nuzzles your ankles, and you reach down to scratch him behind the ears. "Deedee seems to have decided you're not half bad."

You tell Deedee it is nice to meet him, and you shuffle uncertainly. "I..." You look around, at the hanging violet lights and the show flyers tacked to the cupboards. "I don't..."

I take my seat at the chipped table, indicating the spot across from me. "You're wondering why you're here?" You nod, swallowing, and I laugh. "Aren't we all?" I hold out my palm. "The token, if you don't mind?"

"Oh, right," you say, and drop the metal into my hand, where it seems to vanish before you can trace its destination. You sip the tea, find yourself overcome by memories of a home you've never known.

"Rosehip, licorice, and coriander," I say, sipping my own. Deedee hops onto the table, and my slender fingers stroke his arching back. "I would like, if I may, to take you on a strange journey," I grin. "Do you consent?"

You remember the first time you heard those words, pleather-clad and young and dumb and caught in the rain. Head swimming, eyes watering in the perfumed air, you breathe out, almost imperceptibly: "I do."

"Excellent," I say, clapping my hands and standing. You follow the flowing sleeves of my mesh top as I open one of the cupboards, revealing a bookshelf. My fingers dance along leather-clad spines, searching, feeling, scrying, an old familiar patter. "Hope you're cozy. I have a quota to meet, you see."

Before you can ask what I mean, my hand darts out like a snapping turtle, snatches a slender crimson volume from near the bottom of the shelf. I open it gingerly, letting the contents bleed out into the air. As I turn, the scene begins to change, you begin to change and I begin to dissolve into nothing but a musical voice, mingling with the perfume in the air.

"Attend, pilgrim, and beware the murderous milieu before you... One for sorrow, two for joy, three for a girl, four for a boy, five for silver, six for gold, seven for a secret never to be told... Eight for a wish, nine for a kiss, ten for a surprise you should be careful not to miss... and eleven for health. Eleven tales to tell, eleven solemn vows to swear..."

You are falling, falling, falling into my voice, bold black ink in yellow boxes, lightning crashing across a monolithic splash page that is the whole world. My face is a horrid idol on pulped paper, made grotesque by shading as the book in my hand becomes a greeting card.

"Reader beware, you're in for a scare... You dared to tread on consecrated ground, and now you must face our first tale of terror and transformation... a story of afterbirth, or rebirth, of replacement and renewal... a tale born of ground flesh and sour mother's milk, a tale called..."

BIRTHDAY SUIT

Lennox Rex

It started so low—barely perceptible—but the baritone pulse strengthened within seconds, emboldened by a rolling cymbal rain. It left them taut and poised, shards of anticipation under their skin, until the punch of drum snapped them into action.

They seemed out of their own body—out of their own control—as they moved to the cut of the serrated riffs and the insistent, pounding beat, that baritone thrum always in the background. Images flashed through their mind, colorless and gritty, like an arthouse film: dancing bare feet, fluid limbs and sweat-slick hair flicking to and fro as heads tilted back and offered oblivious expressions up to the sky.

Entranced by the sound reverberating through them and their own impulsive movements, they felt at one with the cavorting crowd—part of a mysterious ritual. They could feel something rising. Some unknown, primordial sense—dark and menacing only because of its foreignness. The dance continued, the strange instinct grew and overtook, until he could feel the exhilaration surging through his veins.

He felt good, felt himself.

Eventually, the sawing guitar buzzed into feedback, which faded into nothing, and he stopped as if someone had flipped a switch. He felt pleasantly wrung out as he strode over to his bedroom door. He had to see his flushed, joyous features for himself.

Colleen grinned at her reflection. The confusion and insatiable need to self-analyze had yet to creep in and settle. For now, she only felt good and right in the universe.

The new transfer at school had to be an illusion. There was no other way to explain their ephemeral nature. Their features seemed to shift with the light, flickering in and out—*male, female, androgynous,* and so on. Looking at them, Colleen never could pin down one specific impression. Even stranger still, they seemed to blend in seamlessly, no matter where she spotted them—to have no effect on their surroundings nor to be affected by it themselves. It occurred to Colleen eventually that she might be the only one to see them at all. Anytime she asked, describing them as best she could, she'd be met with puzzled expressions, apologetic shakes of the head, or needlessly harsh speculations on her sanity.

After maddening weeks, bordering on months, of trying to find this mysterious shifter, Colleen happened upon them when she was least expecting it, in the most mundane place: they were loitering outside the Circle K she always passed by on her way home from school. Almost as if they had been waiting for her. Dumbfounded, Colleen came to a sudden halt and stood, blinking, for a long beat before she finally approached. They didn't budge, simply enjoyed a soda, and allowed her to make the first move.

Up close, they didn't shift with the light. They were perfectly solid and present but that still failed to give Colleen a definitive sense of anything. They wore one too many layers of too loose clothes to be able to discern a chest, but Colleen knew full well that their breasts might just be small, like her own. Their face still had a touch too much baby fat, with angles just a bit too soft to look male, but Colleen thought that perhaps they just hadn't started growing into their pubescent changes. Their hair and makeup, of course, were no help. They could be a girl just as easily as they could be a boy that wanted to look cool, like all the pop stars. *Gender bending*, everyone called it. After all, wouldn't Colleen have close-cropped hair just like Annie Lennox, if only she could? If only her parents hadn't decreed that she was far too old to be a tomboy, that it was time for her to finally grow up and become a proper young lady? She absently scowled and reached back to pull the scrunchy out of her hair, putting it around her left wrist like a bracelet and reaching back again to fan out and fidget with her cinnamon waves.

"What are you thinking about so deeply over there?" They pushed off the wall and offered a teasing grin. "I'd hate to think that scowl was meant for me."

Colleen blushed and dropped her gaze away for a moment. "Sorry." She looked back up, sheepish. Her gaze traveled up their body and back down again, slowly, and she chewed on her lower lip in contemplation before finally meeting their gaze. "Can I ask you kind of a rude question?"

The tease was back in their smile as they regarded her silently. Colleen had brushed her hair forward, over one shoulder, and now she finger-combed it anxiously. Goosebumps rose on her skin under their scrutiny. They finally broke the tension with a mirth-filled chuckle. "There's only one way to find out."

Colleen twisted her hair around the fingers of one hand and tugged, to soothe her nerves as she spoke. "Are you a girl or a boy?"

Their smile widened, and their lips parted to show teeth. Their hazel eyes seemed to shine like gold as they leaned in and answered. "Neither." They caught the straw in their mouth and sipped their fountain drink with an affected primness that normally would've made Colleen laugh, if she weren't so stuck on that single word.

Colleen's jaw dropped, and her fingers began to comb and tug faster as she attempted to order and process her thoughts. "Neither?" She shook her head, as if that would help put everything into its proper context. "Is that—" She leaned in now, her face etched with disbelief, but her eyes glinting with hidden hope and excitement. "Can you do that? Be neither?" She frowned when she noticed an older couple throwing them a disapproving look as they walked into the store. Noting her discomfort, they moved a little further down, towards the small field behind the parking lot. Colleen followed gratefully and waited for the conversation to continue.

Once they were comfortably out of earshot, they stopped and turned back to give a small shrug before speaking in a soft yet authoritative tone. "Identity isn't something other people allow. It's something that just is. I'm not a girl or a boy, I'm just. . ."

The way they had trailed off felt to her like an invitation, and she accepted without thought. "A person?"

Colleen took their silence and sly expression for her answer.

"I'm Diana, by the way." They smirked, deeply amused.

A fresh blush bloomed furiously across Colleen's cheeks, and she threw her gaze down to the dying grass. "Oh my God, duh. Sorry!" She shook her head at herself and looked up again, with a shy smile. "Colleen."

Diana took another long sip from their straw, until they both heard the tell-tale *schleerp* of Diana getting down to the last drops of soda. They brought their emptied cup down from their mouth and gave Colleen an unabashedly assessing look. "I've been thinking," they trailed off again, inciting Colleen's curiosity.

"Thinking what?" She began fidgeting with the shoulder straps of her backpack as she waited with an open, eager expression.

"You seem like one of us." They gestured to themselves with their cup. "Like me, I mean. A kindred spirit."

"I'm not—" Colleen stepped back and shrugged, scuffing her shoe on a bald patch of dirt. "I'm not neither."

"Of course not." Diana closed the distance between them and leaned back in. Colleen found herself mirroring the movement, until their foreheads almost touched, and Colleen's hair fell forward like a curtain to keep their conversation private. "But you're definitely not a girl," Diana whispered. "Are you?"

It took Colleen's brain a few minutes to catch up to the conversation. She'd never had someone ask her such a bold question, so plainly. She'd also never met someone who genuinely seemed to care about the answer, not the way she suspected Diana cared. She pulled away, straightening to her full height, then thought better of it and came closer again instead. She brought her mouth as close to Diana's face as possible without whispering in her ear, and spoke in a small, secretive tone. "I don't want to be. I feel wrong this way." She rested her hand on Diana's shoulder without thinking and this time did whisper directly into their ear. "Something's really not right. It's really wrong, and it's suffocating me." She clamped her teeth down on her lower lip and blinked away a tear.

Diana surprised her by wrapping their arms around her and pulling her in for a hug. It was an awkward embrace, with Diana's arms wrapping around her backpack as well and the cup still clutched in their hand, but it made Colleen feel a sudden surge of comfort and security she never would've expected. It was them who whispered in her ear now. "Are you a boy?"

Colleen nodded and instantly buried her face in the crook of Diana's neck, to hide her embarrassment. They shifted, moving their free hand to stroke Colleen's hair, as if to say *shhhhh, it's nothing to be embarrassed of.* She nuzzled her face in deeper still, her flushed skin hot against them, and wondered how exactly she was having such an intimate conversation with a stranger. *But I've been looking for them so long that they don't feel strange.*

"What's your name?"

The gentle encouragement in their tone warmed Colleen's heart. She pulled back, breaking the embrace, but suddenly felt too scared to look them in the eye. "It's- um." She mechanically went about fixing her hair and worrying at her lower lip. Diana waited patiently, until Colleen finally peered up and answered meekly. "Emery. It's Emery."

"Bitchin'!" Diana nodded as if that made it all official, and Colleen's heart lifted. "So, Emery," they grinned, "can we hang later?"

Colleen nearly bounced on the balls of her feet and clapped her hands together in her excitement. Befriending Diana seemed like the most important thing in the world at that moment. She tried not to come across too eager and failed spectacularly. "Oh yeah, totally, like, fer sure!"

Diana chuckled fondly and nodded their affirmation. "I'll show you how to be a boy," they threw out with a mysterious, sly look. They were already well on their way back towards the parking lot by the time Colleen had decided she'd heard what she'd heard, and another sharp realization intruded before she could go after them. *How are we going to hang out if we didn't exchange numbers or anything?*

When she looked again, Diana was somehow already gone.

Colleen opened her eyes to find herself curled up in a warm, moist nest of moss. Allowing her mind time to wake up and figure out where she was, she unfurled her body and gave it a good stretch before standing. She took a few minutes to right herself, pulling small twigs and bits of dead leaf out of her hair. Cool, silvery light allowed her a clear view of a large clearing, surrounded by the sharp, pointed silhouettes of pine trees. *Am I back behind the house*, she asked herself despite knowing she wasn't. She blinked and had to do a double take. In the center of the clearing sat a table, as large and round as the full moon pinned up in the sky; and around it gathered a small group of people, happily chattering amongst themselves. *How did I not notice that?* She took a few tentative steps forward, her bare feet sinking into the supple ground. Just then, someone turned away from the table, and Colleen's mouth curved into a relieved smile when she saw Diana get up and come towards her. They were dressed in a plain tunic now, and sans makeup, but Colleen felt she would've recognized them anywhere.

"Emery, you made it!" They reached her in what seemed like the blink of an eye and pulled her into a tight embrace. "Please, come eat with us!" They guided her to the center of the clearing.

Everyone gathered around the table adjusted to face Collen fully. She looked from blood-smeared face to bloodied smile, the incongruity of the situation forming a fuzzy film of shock over her synaptic bridges. Having satisfied their curiosity, one of the group brought their attention back to what they'd been doing, drawing Colleen's gaze along with them. "Is that—" Her face wrinkled in disgust as she watched them lovingly finger the bluish-white braid that erupted into thick, protruding veins branching out like tree roots across a large lump of meat in a deep shade of bruised purple. "Is that someone's placenta?" As if to punctuate her question, they leaned in and took a bite out of the umbilical cord, severing it from the rest of the afterbirth. They passed along the placenta, chewing on the end of their umbilical treat as if it were merely a stick of jerky.

Diana softened their face and offered an encouraging smile that made their eyes invitingly bright. "You can't create a whole being out of nothing," they pointed out cheerfully. "You must plant a seed."

"This?" Aghast, Colleen eyed the meat on the table one more time. "This is what you meant when you said you'd show me how to be a boy? This is. . . grody." She scrunched up her face and stuck out her tongue in disgust.

Diana rested their hand on her shoulder and moved to murmur into her ear. "What I meant, Emery, is that I can make you a boy." They pulled back so they could look her dead in the eye, and she could see the earnestness in their face. "Literally."

"Literally?" The word fell out of Colleen's mouth in a heavy haze of confusion and skepticism.

"Literally," they repeated. "I can help you become Emery. Like, totally for real." They gave her shoulder a squeeze before letting go and straightening to stand to their full height, which somehow seemed a bit taller than it had been earlier that day. "Don't you want that? You seemed to want it earlier." They shrugged. "Maybe you don't want it enough?"

Panic easily overtook and obliterated all the doubt that had just been gaining traction. She sucked in a deep breath, straightening her spine to stand tall as she did. She held it for a long beat, then let it back out in a sudden rush. "Yeah, I want this." She nodded and took up the last remaining spot at the table. "I really do." She locked gazes with the person to her right and held out her hands, palms up. "I'll eat it."

She had to bite back a groan of distress when they plopped the organ into her hands. It was still warm, and disturbingly mushy. It coated her palms a deep crimson as soon as it made contact. She quickly clenched her eyes shut, to get rid of the visual that was making bile rise in her esophagus, and tried to ignore the metallic scent that was so strong she could taste pennies on the back of her tongue. *Just do it, already,* she scolded herself. *One.* She paused, needing to force her muscles to relax. *Two.* She took another centering breath. *Three.*

Keeping her eyes closed, she took a bite. The organ squished between her teeth, giving easily when she used her canines and incisors to tear and pull. Her portion slid onto her tongue in a burst of bitter warmth, the iron-rich blood coating the inside of her cheeks, making them sting. Her mind projected a subtle, sickening *squelch* against her ear drums as her molars ground up the mass of tissue and blood vessels. It fell down her gullet like jelly after only a brief chewing.

She opened her eyes to find herself shivering in the cool night air, huddled into herself on the forest floor. Her nightshirt had bloody fingerprints from where she clutched herself with blood-slick hands, and the taste of placenta was still fresh on her tongue.

After that, Colleen only ever saw Diana in dreams—if they were truly dreams; the way she always woke up to find herself laying in the woods back behind her house left her with only questions. She wasn't offered anymore organ meat after that first visit to the clearing. Instead, they all danced. Sweat-soaked skin, oblivious minds, and bodies possessed by the insistent beat—the kind of wild, free dancing that always made Emery feel right within himself and within the universe, made him forget all about that girl named Colleen.

Soon enough, Colleen once again woke up in her mossy bed to see the round table in the center of the clearing with the gossamer light of the full moon lending the scene a certain magic. Diana came to meet her with something held carefully in their hands. "Drink this." They thrust a simple earthen cup into her hands by way of greeting.

She brought it up towards her face, but paused when a strange odor reached her nose. Just underneath a potent musk, she could detect faint scents of blood and bleach. Her nose wrinkled in distaste, pulling the corners of her mouth wide in a tight, skeptical line. "What is this, Diana?"

"Do the details really matter?" Diana offered a sweet expression and gave her shoulder a reassuring squeeze. "Think of it as a vitamin smoothie. Needed nutrients." They patted her belly. "You can't plant a seed and never water it."

Colleen cocked her head, eyeing them dubiously.

Diana chuckled in amusement. "You need to trust me." They nodded encouragingly when Colleen brought the cup closer, resting its rim up against the seam of her lips. "Don't worry about what it is, just what it will do for you."

At last, she parted her lips and tilted the cup, gulping down as much as she could in one swallow. The regret was nearly instantaneous, and it took all she had not to let the cup fall from her hands and shatter on the ground. The revolting combination of mineral-ly, sweet, salty, and ever so slightly bitter made her shiver as she kept herself from choking it back up by sheer force of will. She coughed, as if that could somehow get the taste out of her mouth, and shoved the cup back towards Diana, who took it with gentle patience. "Why was it warm," Colleen gasped, "and that thickness. . ." She shivered again. "Kind of like snot. Please tell me I don't need to drink it all!"

"Of course not," Diana rubbed her back soothingly, "you drank enough. It takes some getting used to, I know."

"I don't want to get used to that!" Colleen spat. She met Diana's placid expression with a sneer. "Is this some kind of joke? Totally bogus!"

Diana's face fell sadly for a moment before they pulled it back together into a look of exasperation. "No need to get nasty." Their voice was tight, taking her by surprise and tempering her anger. "This is a process, Girl." Colleen cringed. Of all things, having *girl* thrown in her face was the reaction she'd expected least—truthfully, not at all. She bit down hard on her bottom lip to keep herself from pointing out how cruel that had felt. Diana took a step closer, seeming to loom over Colleen with a startlingly cold gaze. "You can have what you want, Emery. Be who you should be, but only if you're truly willing. It doesn't seem like you are. Seems like you're the one treating this as a joke. An ancient rite of the liminal. You think you know better than us?"

"Better than us? What does that mean?" The ground seemed to slip away, out from under her feet, while her brain scrambled to process her thoughts and decode information. She finally snapped her mouth shut and regarded Diana with a new sense of trepidation. "You—you're not human, are you?"

Diana closed their eyes and heaved a heavy sigh. Their lips moved as they counted their breaths silently, regaining their composure. "I think the word you really mean is *mortal*, and the answer there would be 'obviously not.' That's hardly relevant, though." They opened their eyes and relaxed their face. Their tone was once again light and patient. "I'm an agent of change, Emery. Nothing more and nothing less. If change is what you want, I am happy to guide you through the ways of my kin, but you need to trust me. Unconditionally." Their mouth was a firm line and their face completely locked down as they waited for a response.

"I'm sorry, Diana!" Colleen frantically ran her fingers through her hair, unconsciously fluffing it as she struggled to fully display the depths of her remorse. "I don't mean to be ungrateful or disrespectful or—" She groped for the right word, but gave up with a sharp shrug. "... ignorant. . . or whatever. Please, help me. Let me keep going. I'll do whatever it takes! Totally whatever it takes!" She implored Diana with desperate eyes, tugging on their hand with both hands, rather than reaching out to clutch at Diana's arms like she really wanted to.

"If that's what you want," Diana replied coolly, "but we're finished for tonight."

When Colleen came to in the woods, her face was wet with tears.

The Process, as Diana had called it, continued smoothly from that point on. Colleen drank and ate whatever was offered to her without complaint and danced with joyful abandon. After a while, she noticed that her period had synched with her dreams of the clearing, and she could only wonder when exactly that had happened, just as she wondered if her dream meals had anything to do with how heavy and painful her periods had become.

Colleen groaned in pain and hunched down in her chair, taking a moment to ride out the cramp that tore through her like an earthquake.

"My poor baby." Her mother reached over and stroked her hair tenderly. "And here I thought you might be lucky." She shook her head sadly. "Just like all the Ralston women. I'm sorry it hurts, Sweetheart."

Colleen managed to throw her a grateful look even as she whimpered. "Thanks, Mom," she said weakly once the pain had passed.

Her father let his fork clatter against his plate as he glared at them and gave a disapproving *harumph*. "Save all this period talk for later. It's hardly appropriate for a nice family dinner."

Colleen mumbled a half-hearted "Sorry, Dad," while her mother rolled her eyes in an obvious, exaggerated manner before giving her husband an especially sweet smile and patting his thigh. "Excuse us, Dear." She turned back to Colleen, who had gone back to her plate with relish. "I must say, Sweetie, you sure have an appetite these days."

Her father laughed. "Eating us out of house and home. Do we have a daughter or a son?"

Unamused, Colleen would only go as far as smiling at his joke. She barely held back a cringe when she felt a ripple of movement across her abdomen. "Ummm, excuse me, please." She shot up from the table and lurched towards the hall. She could hear her mother sadly muttering "my poor baby" as she hurried to her room. Once inside, she curled up into a ball atop her bed and buried her face into her pillow. Right on cue, she felt more movement inside herself, followed by a cramp so painful, she nearly blacked out as she screamed into her pillow.

Later that night, in the clearing, she told everyone all about her dinner, but everyone seemed pleased and excited for her, rather than sympathetic. Diana clapped their hands together and nearly shouted. "Soon! It's going to happen so soon!"

"What's gonna happen?" Colleen grabbed their arm and gave their bicep a light squeeze. "What's happening to my body, Diana?"

Rather than answer, Diana took her by both arms and started them spinning. "Just dance," they said. "Let's dance together." Soon enough, Colleen had forgotten everything. She danced, spinning in tighter and tighter circles, wearing tracks into the ground, until a cramp hit her, taking her down as if she'd been shot. She writhed on the ground, growling and whimpering in agony, forgetting everything but the persistent, throbbing tear of pain radiating up from the angry slash of her vaginal opening. Once everything had finally faded away, leaving her panting for breath, she found herself back in her own woods, dirt and twigs tangled in her hair, and blood thick on her inner thighs. She carefully stood up and limped back to the house, where she sobbed silently in the shower.

⚨

The word *soon* echoed in her head, in Diana's most delighted voice, as Colleen finally reached her house. The 10-minute walk home from school had felt more like days. The nurse had offered to call her mother at her volunteer job, but Colleen had insisted she could make it home fine. She could only laugh at herself now. She would, too, if only she weren't in such distress. She hoped that *soon* was really coming up as fast as Diana believed, because she couldn't take many more periods like this.

Clutching her abdomen, Colleen lunged forward into the house. She mindlessly shoved the front door closed behind herself but didn't notice if it had shut and didn't bother to check either. She was ready to drop to the floor with a loud thud, right alongside her backpack when she shrugged it off her shoulders. A new sharp shock of pain yanked a startled shout out of her, and she resisted the urge to double over. She had to get to her bedroom. She was only a few steps down the hall when she changed her mind. The thought of being inside, being confined, was too much. *This is too much pain. I need space.* She changed direction and staggered into the living room, out through the glass

— 15 —

sliding door, across the unfenced yard, past the tree line and into the woods, where she finally allowed herself to drop down in a squirming heap.

She grunted in heavy disgust when she felt an especially large, thick blood clot about to pass. Oddly, it seemed to stop halfway, as if stuck, and then there was another of the blinding, heart-stopping cramps she'd been experiencing ever since her first meal at Diana's table. The sounds of the forest around her, the grit of the dirt, rocks, and twigs under her, even the air's cheery smell—it all disappeared as all the pain seized all her senses. She sucked in as deep a breath as her lungs could manage and curled into herself. She tensed every muscle group, to keep herself still until the pain passed. For the first time, it didn't. Instead, she could've sworn that hands slid down along her inner walls and fingernails dug into the slick, bloody flesh before those hands began to push apart with all their might.

Even as her breath came rushing out in a tortured yelp, Colleen felt compelled to help. She unfurled herself, wincing in agony, and pulled off her skirt and underwear. Laying on her back, oblivious to the way blood seeped down her perineum and mixed with the loose soil to form a paste that clung to her skin, she took a few long, shaky breaths to ready herself. As prepared as she'd ever be, she reached down, slipped four trembling fingers inside herself—two on either side—and began to pull. The whimpers and howls that erupted from her mouth as she felt her pelvis fracture and rip were as inhuman as the primal, animalistic growls and grunts she emitted from the effort of rending herself apart. Her own tears blinded her, and her lips had been bitten and punctured, chewed completely raw by the time she blessedly lost consciousness.

Emery emerged from the human wreckage with a determined shout, using his fingers and nails once again to grab hold, dig in, and pull until he was sliding forward in a burst of blood, bile, urine, and mucus. Despite the open air and seemingly endless pines, Emery could pick out only a coppery scent so strong its warm, moist tang coated his tongue. "Ugh, it's like a full pad first thing in the morning," he muttered. He cracked his eyes open and immediately shut them again with a pained hiss. His hands were sullied with blood and dirt, so he turned back and groped about until he found his discarded skirt. He cleaned off his face and hands as well as he could and took in a deep breath of

Christmas-scented air as he blinked his surroundings into slow focus. Ignoring the pile of flesh for the time being, he peered ahead, through the trees. The house was still easy to see, so he must not have made it very far before his pain overwhelmed him.

He sat and listened, appreciating the sounds of life surrounding him: birdsong, the buzz of insects flying past, the occasional twig snap or parting ferns as a small animal moves through. Eventually, he stood, and a short shiver of sharp excitement traveled up his spine as the perfectly cool spring air breezed against his freshly exposed groin. Laughing, he peered down at himself, and couldn't help the urge to reach down and cradle his slippery sac, recoating his hands in the waxy white secretion that covered his body. His eyes shined with tears and wonder as he tentatively tugged on his penis—giving it one slow, exploratory stroke—and watched himself start to harden. "Wow," he murmured in a delightfully deep voice. A little reluctantly, he let go of himself to run his hands up his torso, from his hips up to his clavicles, and down again. "So flat." He laughed again, feeling a little giddy when he brought his hands to rest on his pectorals. "I'm so flat."

"Happy Birthday, Emery."

He turned towards the familiar voice, his lips already broadening into an ecstatic grin. "Hey, Diana!" His hands continued to travel unconsciously up and down, side to side, back and forth. He made no attempt to hide himself, or his obvious excitement, and Diana in turn made nothing of it. They merely returned his joy with a gleeful smile of their own.

"It's nice to meet you as you truly are," they offered.

The two of them stood in place, beaming at each other, for a long beat before Diana moved towards the carcass behind him, opening a burlap sack they'd been holding in one hand. "Just let me grab this," they said absently.

"You're taking it?" He watched them fit the opening of the bag over one end of his former self and begin to carefully shimmy it over the rest of the mangled remains.

Diana didn't pause as they spoke in their reassuringly authoritative tone. "You'll still need her, especially as you go through these first stages of transition." They closed the sack, heaved it up over their shoulder as if it weighed nothing, and stood. "Alright, let's go, Emery."

He looked around, not terribly keen on walking through the forest naked, and picked up his now filthy skirt. "Better than nothing," he thought aloud as he pulled it on, loving the sound of his new voice. He nodded at Diana. "I'm ready for what's next. Lead the way."

Lighting strikes again, and you blink, and you're here once more, and I'm here, and that light little smile pirouettes an my painted lips as the book rejoins its brethren.

"What…?" you begin, shaking your head, and then quiet yourself, reaching for your tea instead. Your questions feel foolish. You understand as well as you can what has happened, what is happening, what is about to happen again.

"It's always a little disorienting your first time," I assure you. "But you'll get the hang of it before our night is out." That sweet smile turns into something leering, almost lecherous if it weren't for the mirth and good cheer caught between my teeth. "Did you think you were here for a shag?"

You blush.

"If you stay such a captive audience, it's not out of the question," I wink, leaving the bookshelf and opening the minifridge. You see a steak, salted but entirely rare, on what appears to be a novelty McDonald's *plate featuring* Disney's *Megara.*

"Eat," I ay, placing it before you.

You open your mouth to protest, but then smell the copper tang in air, feel your saliva squirt into the cavern of your mouth, and then your fingers are reaching for the meat. There is no coercion in the act; you find you want this carnal indulgence, realize you have never once tasted bloody muscle in all your years of grinding carrion between your teeth.

"Our second tale, a tale of actualization and consumption, of fur and fang, of skin and bones and a broken home… Dig in, pilgrim… Dig in, dine upon this grisly mosel. I know you hunger for…"

FRESH MEAT

Thea Maeve

⋔

Drained by my thoughts, I turned off the music and drove in silence. The freeway was devoid of other cars, leaving me with nothing but space and time. A police van idled on the shoulder, but I had no need to speed. I had nowhere to go. With nothing else to do, I veered off a random exit. The street I chose was decorated with neon signs advertising Girls! and Topless! and further down was exactly what my impulses desired: Wawa.

In the handicapped spot sat a Ford F-150 with sun spots on the hood. My throat thirsted for iced tea to wash the itch building at the base of my tongue. That itch freaked me out, because I couldn't be sure if it was real or in my head. Nonetheless, I waited, paranoid of being spotted, as if eye contact would reveal everything about me to a stranger. A dog jogged across the front of the store, stopping momentarily to glance at me. We locked eyes. It looked familiar, but stray dogs are everywhere in the city these days. Finally, a young man wearing a camo jacket, jeans, and *Phillies* hat left the store. The dog bolted in the opposite direction, into the darkness beside the building. By the time I turned around, the man had already pulled out of the parking lot. I was alone.

Immediately upon stepping through the door, I regretted going there, but it was too late. The fresh scents of bread comforted my nose, and the bright lights illuminated the soft color scheme of reds and browns and yellows inside. It was all too normal for this experience. I should have chosen a 7/11 or something I didn't frequent much at all. The cashier barely noticed me. He was stacking dip in the shelves behind the counter, and let me browse in peace. I made my way to the iced tea section, and picked blackberry flavor because I usually picked peach and needed something different. On my way to the counter, I thought to get some jerky, but figured that was too sexual, so I chose chips instead.

"Was it good?" The cashier stared at me from the counter, ready to check me out. How did he know? I looked down at my shirt to see if there were any stains or noticeable signs. Do men get marked differently when we suck a dick for the first time? No. That was silly. The "gaydar" is just a silly joke.

"Is that all?" He said, checking out my items.

"Yes." I couldn't tell if he'd asked if it was good, prying into my sex life, the first of many such questions, no doubt. Or was I hearing things?

"$3.67" He said.

I pulled out my wallet and paid, then rushed out of there. The cashier, I noticed, resumed stacking the shelves. Back in the safety of my Sonata, I cracked open the iced tea and knocked back half the bottle, letting the blackberry flavor push the itch down my throat. When breathing, I moved my tongue around, wondering if it was still there, and I could have sworn it was. So I chugged the rest, sat, and cried.

It was as if I'd swallowed a parasite, resting on my uvula, teasing me to swallow more. There was no spitting or puking it out. It was there, forever feasting on me. What would the doctor think? I chuckled a bit at that, but it brought me back to the realization of how hidden this must remain. My parents could never find out. My friends could never find out. Nobody could ever find out.

I turned on the music, desperate for distraction; Red Velvet sang about being little monsters. Even though I didn't know a word of Korean, I mimicked the words as best as I could. The city lights blended together into neon blues and yellows as I drove through the side streets. What lurked in the darkness between the city lights and the stars and myself and Red Velvet was something I tried my best to forget.

The sun stared at me and I hated it. It was too hot. Too bright. Every morning, I woke up later and later. Every night, I stayed awake later and later. I often stared at the moon: fascinating and pure, and so unlike the sun. The moon sat in the sky, present, but unobtrusive. As opposed to the sun's relentless attack, the moon was cool and soothing, like a gentle mother rocking me in her arms. So long as the moon existed, I existed. Instead, at the moment, it was the harsh sun with its judgment. BreathingOpening my mouth to breathe in this heat was like prying my tongue from the desert of my mouth so I could pant for a few seconds.

I closed my mouth when I noticed my mother looking at me.

"Would you like anything to drink while the cooler's open?" My mom asked.

"Sure. I'll have a beer," I said.

My dad and uncle were discussing the stray dog infestation, as they put it, in the city. They figured we need more pounds in the city to get them off the streets. He was taken aback when my mom disturbed their conversation by handing him a beer.

"Here, pass this down to Steve." She handed the beer to my dad, who decided to toss it over to me. I caught it but now it was shaken, so I buried it halfway into the sand next to my feet and went back to ignoring everybody.

The ocean created soothing white noise in the background, like a sweet song wrapping me in a blanket. I reflected back to a week ago, driving around Philadelphia after my meeting with Patrick. I thirsted for that night, like my soul was anchored there by my new parasitic organ. I remembered the thrill of sliding my hands down his hairy chest and abs until my lipstick touched his manhood. His wild green eyes staring down at me, filled with lust and fire.

The sun reminded me I was hot and sweaty. The thoughts weren't helping. Flashes of that night, where flesh and blood congealed into one blurry image, gave me a headache.

I cracked open the *Bud Light* and took a large gulp.

"Steve." The sound of my name disturbed me. It was my mom looking at me. "Aunt Georgia wants to know what you've been reading lately."

"I see you are always posting new books on Instagram and it is amazing that you read so much. I'm surprised you don't have a book in your hands right now." My aunt was smiling at me.

"I haven't felt much like reading lately. Taking a break, I guess." It was as good an answer as any. And it was true, too. I hadn't read a book since before that night. It wasn't a conscious decision; I didn't know if I had any conscious decisions anymore. There was simply no escape from my thoughts, in a book or a movie or a poem or a song. I took another gulp of my beer, which was sour as it went down.

"Oh Steve, your nose." My mom squinted to look closer. "It's bleeding."

I ran my finger up to my nose to check, and sure enough, it was painted red. My mom reached into the cooler to pull out a bottle of water. I put my finger in my mouth and sucked on the blood. It tasted sweet and savory: much better than the beer.

"Here, this should help." My aunt pulled a paper towel out of her cooler and handed it to my mother. She was walking over to me now, the water and towel in hand, as I coated my finger with more blood.

"Put this on your nose to stop the bleeding." She handed me the paper towel and the water bottle.

"Thanks. It's not a big deal."

"I can't believe this. How did you start bleeding?"

"Must have been the sun." I shrugged. "It's so hot out."

I put my finger back in my mouth and slurped on my blood. It brought me back to that night, in the basement of Patrick's house in the dark. A fresh taste in my mouth, disgusting and delicious. New boundaries unfolded.

My mom stared at me oddly, so I pressed the paper towel to my nose.

"Thanks," I said.

Satisfied with herself, she took her seat again.

My mouth salivated for the blood. After some time, when I figured the blood had stopped flowing, I stuck my tongue out and slid the bloody paper towel across it. It was so pleasurable. I lifted my other hand up to my nose and now the other nostril was bleeding.

I stood up; sand kicked onto my uncle as my feet lifted. The beer can tipped onto its side, spilling its contents into the sand. No great loss, I thought. Maybe the crabs could get wasted.

"Oh honey, are you okay?" Aunt Georgia asked. "Your nose is still bleeding."

"Yeah, I think I am gonna call it a day and go back to the house." I started putting on my flip flops.

"It's just a nose bleed. I'm sure it will stop soon," my father said.

"It's too hot anyway. I want to sit in the air conditioning."

"We'll be right behind you shortly, I'm sure," my mom said. She side-eyed my father. "It's very hot."

"Right, well, take the chair with you." My father crossed his arms and laid back in his own chair.

"Alright." I lifted the chair and my towel and started lugging them across the beach to go to the house. During my walk, my nose continued to bleed, and the trail reached my mouth. I licked the blood from my lips and the savory flavor sent a renewed energy through my body. I hurried home, nearly jogging with the chair on my shoulder. When I got home, I turned on the outdoor hose and sprayed down my feet, then my hands. I dropped the chair in the garage and escaped into the house, then to my bedroom.

I rushed my hands to my nose, rubbing them in the fresh blood emerging there and then shoving them into my mouth, devouring, gulping it all down. When the blood started running dry, I panicked, needing more than I had received. I squeezed the top of my nose to get more to leak out. It worked, fresh blood splashed onto my fingers and I spent a few more minutes slurping it up until finally, pinching the bridge of my nose as tight as I could resulted in no more blood.

It was all dried up. Confused, and aroused, I turned my attention elsewhere. Sweet relief washed over my body. My blood-stained fingers coated my cock red. Patrick flashed into my vision, hairy and tall. He took me back to that night where he guided me to his bedroom, and I relived the twinge of his teeth upon my lips as he bit me. We slid beneath the covers and he loved me, soft and caring, then hard and ravaging in an animalistic rage. He was beyond a man to me—a hero, an immortal, a god.

I came on the floor; the white cum mixed with my red blood in a glorious splatter across the laminate wood. I knelt to lick that up too, and the salty bitter liquid taste washed over my tongue: familiar and wonderful.

The patio door slid open and I pulled up my pants and rushed into the bathroom across the hall.

"Steve, you okay?" My mom asked.

I stared at myself in the mirror. My nose swelled bright red. There was some cum above my mouth. I licked it up, then turned on the sink and washed my face.

"Steve?"

After a deep breath, I looked in the mirror again. My body heaved up and down in a steady rhythm with my breath. To my surprise, there was no disappointment, no disgust, no shame. I made eye contact with myself exhilarated by the thrill we shared. The deep blues of my irises shone brighter than the sun, like they captured all the beauty of the Earth into one small blue hole. I smiled wide, almost wickedly but not quite. It was the grin of somebody who knew what they wanted and knew they were in control. My true self was liberated.

"I'm great," I said.

The rest of vacation was spent finding moments to masturbate, thinking of my night in Philadelphia. During our ride back to the city, the trees grew thicker as we came closer to the vast woods of Pennsylvania. We crossed the Delaware River where the lights of Philadelphia awaited us, and I realized that there was no going back to who I was, for better or worse. In the sky, the moon looked down upon me, as if to nod its approval. Somewhere in that silent conversation, we decided together, the moon and I, that my change was permanent and could not be hidden. I cried silently to myself, the hair on my skin raising into an emotional crescendo. Desperately, I wanted to jump out of the car and give chase until I could wrap my arms around the moon, and sink my teeth deep into her flesh.

"Steve, are you okay?" My mom asked. "You're breathing deeply."

"Yeah, mom. I'm fine." She ruined my moment.

"You look sick and you've been quieter than normal. Are you sure?" She was looking at me in the reflection of her makeup mirror.

"Yeah."

"Is there something on your face?" She turned in her seat.

"No." I said.

"It looks like you're growing a beard."

"I shaved this morning." I touched my face and there wasn't stubble; instead there was a short beard that my fingers burrowed through. As I pulled my arms down, I noticed the hair growing longer and darker on them as well with the skin becoming less visible beneath their growth.

"Are you okay?" my mom asked.

My entire body emblazoned into a deep, eternal itch. I clawed at my body, digging my nails into my skin, burying them deep to find a way to turn the itch off. It was over my arms, my legs, my chest, my back, inside my brain, poking at my cerebrum with a crazed frenzy.

"Steve!" My dad screeched as I kicked the back of his chair. I didn't mean to do it. My body was acting on its own accord, responding to the deep irritation tearing at my veins.

I did my best to keep up, scratching my arms, my chest, and when I reached for my legs, I pierced my skin entirely. The iron scent of blood filled the car, as I dug further, drawing more and more until my legs were painted red.

"What's is wrong?" My mom cried. "Frank, we need to get him to a hospital."

The car sped up, so did my claws. They worked tirelessly digging through my growing hairs, stabbing deep into my skin. The seat belt came undone as I kicked again, and my body floundered on the backseat. The cloth seats were like thorns against my skin. Then I bent forward and slurped the blood of my wounds. It was like an orgasm, my toes curling, and my head growing light.

"Calm down. We just have a few exits until..." I slammed my fist on the back of my dad's seat, and in the middle of my fury, I locked eyes with the moon. I needed to get out, into the night and the fresh air. Away from my family. I kicked hard at the window, confident I could break it.

"Steve! Stop!" My mom was hemorrhaging tears now. But I couldn't tell if she was my mother anymore. I was not Steve anymore. I was nobody. I was a beast launching myself at the glass. I was the darkness between the stars and the city lights.

The glass shattered into a million pieces. Tires screeched. Metal crunched. Teeth rattled. My head slammed hard into the roof of the car, but it didn't hurt me much. Then the car flipped and collapsed in on itself. The hood scraped along the pavement, grinding my ear drums until the car stopped sliding.

Then there was silence. I sucked in the air, swallowing as much as I could. It tasted like gasoline. The itching and the pain subsided, leaving only a deep craving within my soul. New smells rushed into my nose: burnt rubber, anti-freeze, brake fluid, asphalt, pollution, blood, meat, bone.

Next to me was the shattered front windshield. I glanced the other way where my mother and father hung upside down in their seats like animal corpses in a butcher's warehouse. Blood dripped from my father's forehead; my mom made a soft, constant humming sound. They were both alive. I didn't want to eat them; that would be gross.

"Goodbye," I said. I gave each of them a kiss on the forehead. "You did your best." My mom's eyes opened momentarily and shut again. Without further ceremony, I scrunched through the windshield and disappeared off the highway into the city streets below.

⚬

The city lights glimmered as I walked through South Philadelphia. The car accident had been close to where I-95 passed the stadiums. My arm was still bleeding, which intensified my hunger. A jogger was approaching—young, tall, and handsome. I sprinted at him. It was the fastest I had ever run in my life. A wild terror shone in his eyes. He turned to run the other way, but it was too late. My fangs dug deep into his neck and bit through his artery. He screamed for a moment, kicking and punching then lay still. I spared little time swallowing all his juicy meat. It burst in my mouth, wet and sloppy, and I slid it down my throat until my stomach was full. It was rejuvenating. My wounds were healed, my head a little lightheaded as if I could fly through the streets.

I was on all fours now, my footsteps as quick as my heartbeat. Humans saw me running through the streets. I likely appeared to them as some cross between a great dane and a pitbull. It would be difficult for them to narrow down a breed, but what came to their heads would be a mean bitch—and that was good enough for me. So long as they stayed out of my way, I wouldn't be forced to expose their skeletons to the world.

The streets blurred across my vision. The air filled with beastly aromas: drool, blood, piss, semen, fangs, hair. I could smell the darkness of them: my found family. Down in the dirty grime beneath the city, beneath the subways, beneath the sewage, they paced tirelessly waiting for my arrival. The scents carved my path through the city streets guiding me home.

I was in a state of pure bliss, as if my mind was floating among the stars, and my arms hugged the moon tightly. I had never experienced joy comparable to that moment of unrelenting freedom, like running wild through a forest to hunt and play for the first time.

It wasn't long before I stood in front of an ancient building in the middle of Old City. It was all aged brick, with stairs flanked by gargoyles baring their fangs. It reeked of blood and lust: my family.

I walked up and knocked on the red door. After a few seconds, a metal plate in the middle slid to the side. A gentleman who smelled like pine and moss appeared.

"Password?"

"Accalia," I said.

Then the metal plate slammed closed and the door opened wide.

"Welcome home," he said.

I strolled in, still very much a dog. The walls were covered in beautiful vibrant paintings of wild beasts in various activities: playing in fields, feasting in forests, dancing in clubs, fighting in bars. All were naked in their violence and glory.

"What is your name?" The gentleman put his hand on my shoulder.

I wished I had thought of a new name on the way here, since Steve was dead, but it bounced onto my tongue as if it was natural to me.

"Stephanie," I said.

"Stephanie, I am the pack leader. My name is Romulus. Welcome to Accalia. This way, please." He held my hand and escorted me to the basement door. As it opened, I heard the low growling of my new community. We walked down into the darkness filled with the scent of sweat and pleasure.

"Everyone, this is Stephanie. Stephanie, this is everyone."

I walked into the center of the room. There was a brief pause as they smelled me, and I smelled them. The air was filled with bark and grass, skin and fur, sweat and blood, drool and teeth. Patrick was there, his scent irresistible. He descended upon me and we wrestled. Our tails whipped each other's legs. Our claws gripped each other's fur. Our teeth gnawed each other's necks. We huffed and puffed, groaned and moaned, panted and howled in the deep darkness below the city. Blood splattered across the floor and the walls and the ceiling, painting the room a dark crimson red. My indoctrination lasted for hours and by the end, when my body was spent, I was fulfilled. We lay on the floor, our limbs tumbled over each other. With exasperated breaths, our scents swelled in the air. I was free. I was alive. I was…

"... home," I finish, watching you carefully as reality again resolves itself. "And so, every dog really does have her day, it seems."

You see that the plate before you is empty, and you gulp down the rest of the tea, as if you can hide the shame lining your esophagus behind a curtain of floral accoutrement. And yet... the embarrassment at the baseness of your consumption seems to excite you, and you look at me with hungry eyes, ready for more.

Juice pools on the cartoon face of the woman Heracles killed in a rage, the part they don't show you in the animated musical. Deedee hops onto the table and is all too happy to lick up your leftovers, and your stomach flips as you realize you want to snatch the plate away from the little vermin and make it shine yourself.

There is a tapping at the window, a rapping at my chamber door, not faint at all but loud and sharp. As I open the screen, a stately magpie flutters inside, lighting upon the table.

Within their beak is a scroll, tied with a lilac ribbon, and they look at you expectantly with their little beetle eyes. Trembling, your fingers reach out and take the scroll from the beak, holding it out to me.

As I take it the knot falls open and the scroll unfurls, seeming to stretch longer and longer as the world turns to parchment and print once again. "Allow me to introduce our next yarn, a story of retribution and resolution... a cawing call, a story about how..."

DEATH TAUGHT ME HOW TO LIVE

Alicia Hilton

A

I had fried eggs for breakfast, the last eggs I would ever eat, and followed my brother into the woods. Cougars and wolves did most of their hunting at night, but I'd wrapped the cut on my arm with a thick bandage, so predators wouldn't smell the blood.

Gus reached the creek and stopped. I hung back behind him, watching water rush over the rocks. The waterline had risen, and the smell of fresh rain lingered in the air from a thunderstorm we'd had last night.

Something rustled in the willow tree.

When I looked up, I saw leathery wings and a pointed snout. I figured it was a bat since there were no feathers, but then the head rotated.

Beady eyes peered at us. The beak opened and *hissed.*

Gus picked up a rock that was the size of a hen's egg. "Huck it at the ugly buzzard."

"I don't want to."

"Don't be a sissy." He grabbed my wounded arm and tugged me closer.

Pain made my eyes water. I'd gotten cut when I was helping Gus repair the barbed wire fence that separated our farm from the neighbor's property.

The stone was cool. I threw it, and missed the bald bird on purpose. I was scrawny for a twelve-year-old, but not a klutz.

The bird opened its beak and said, "All who see me laugh me to scorn. Toss another stone, your arm shall be shorn."

Gus said, "Holy crap! The buzzard can *talk.*"

The bird said, "You're ugly buzzards. I am a raven, the mightiest bird in the sky."

All of a sudden, the wind died and the creek stopped gurgling. I heard the *rat, tat, tat* of a woodpecker mining for grubs in a nearby oak tree; otherwise, the woods were unnaturally quiet.

Gus picked up a bigger piece of basalt and hurled it like he was pitching a baseball. The stone struck the bald bird with a *thwack*.

Instead of plummeting to the ground, the raven dove from the tree. Its wings sounded like sheets flapping on a clothesline as it flew towards me.

Claws scraped my temple and plucked a clump of hair and skin. My scalp burned like it had been doused with boiling water, but my screams didn't drown out the bird's taunts.

The raven said, "Packs of dogs encircle me. Vile curs, how dare you stare and gloat over me?"

Gus ran when the bird chased him, but the beast was faster. It lifted its tail and released a gelatinous greenish-white missile that splattered my brother's throwing hand.

I sprinted down the path that led to our cottage. Glancing over my shoulder, I saw Gus grab a rock that was bigger than his fist.

The bird shat on his face.

Gus hollered, stumbled backwards, and fell in the mud. "I can't see. Help me," he said.

The raven soared towards a cluster of evergreens.

I pulled off my shirt and ran to Gus.

The bird crap reeked like rancid meat and had an oily sheen. The horrid smell made my stomach churn, but I scrubbed my brother's face until the slimy mess was almost gone.

Gus opened his eyes. "Thanks, Pete." He walked to the creek, washed his face, and stood. He said, "We'd better get going."

I was looking for the raven and hadn't noticed that the sun had climbed higher in the sky. If my brother didn't hurry, he'd be late clocking in at the sawmill. Our family's money was tight since Father died from cancer, so Gus worked the night shift after he got home from high school, and he worked a full day on Saturdays.

Gus ran past me. His legs were too long for me to keep up.

When I reached our farmhouse, my brother's Ford Bronco was pulling out of the driveway. The truck backfired, making a sound like a gunshot. It was bought used and had a lot of miles on the odometer.

The raven pursued the truck, screeching insults.

Blood seeped from my scalp where the bird had torn out hair, but only a small patch of flesh was gone. I hurried towards the barn. Our cow needed to be milked, the chickens fed, and there were weeds in the vegetable garden, waiting to be plucked.

The next time I saw Gus, he was unconscious in the hospital, his right hand gone, the stump swaddled in bandages.

After he was released from the hospital, neighbors visited, bringing covered dishes.

I stuffed myself with casseroles and pies, but Gus had no appetite for anything except beer.

Every night, Mother and I read the Bible aloud. Gus didn't join us at the table, but he left his bedroom door ajar, and I'd begun to hope that he found inspiration from the scripture.

Nine days into our vigil my eyes were tired, the text blurring, when a gust of wind from an open window ruffled the pages, flipping them so vigorously I almost dropped the heavy leather-bound book.

As quickly as the wind had started, it stopped, leaving an eerie silence. Even the crickets, serenading us from outside, had grown quiet. I had planned to read from *Matthew* next, but the Bible was now open to *Isaiah*.

Mother said, "Shall I read?"

"No, let me." Since *Isaiah* 41:10 was one of my favorite passages, it brought a smile to my face. I said, "So do not fear; I am with you; do not be dismayed, for I am your God. I will strengthen you and help you; I will uphold you with my righteous right hand."

Gus yelled, "Shut up!" He trudged towards us, unsteady on his feet. He said, "Righteous right hand. Very funny."

Tears made my eyes sting. "I'm sorry," I said. "I didn't think."

Mother shoved her chair backward, and stood. "You lost a hand, not your life! Quit feeling sorry for yourself."

My brother's shoulders shook. It was the only time I saw him cry.

Six weeks after the saw blade sliced through Gus's arm, he graduated from high school.

College was no longer an option, since Gus had lost the baseball scholarship. An amputee couldn't pitch or swing a bat.

Our uncle offered Gus the assistant manager position in his sporting goods store in Reno, nearly three hundred miles from our home in Oregon.

Mother smiled when Gus said he'd gotten the job, but the expression didn't reach her eyes. She said, "When'll you leave?"

"Tomorrow," Gus said. He glanced towards the sound of flapping wings.

The bald raven had landed on the porch railing.

Gus turned as white as a sheet.

The raven waved its right foot and said, "Toss another stone, your arm shall be shorn."

I helped Gus pack his suitcase. As I folded shirts and rolled up socks, I felt a weird mixture of relief and guilt. My brother and I had never been close. It wasn't just the age gap. Gus wasn't a jerk, but we didn't have much in common. Whenever he'd tried to push me into becoming like him, I felt insecure.

Gus was an extrovert, big-boned, athletic, and had a string of girlfriends. Maybe I'd overcome my shyness and wouldn't look like a beanpole when I got older, but I probably had a better chance of getting hit by a meteor than becoming captain of the high school baseball team and student body president, like Gus. Pretending that I was interested in girls was harder than faking that I liked sports. If both of us hadn't inherited our father's green eyes, I would've wondered if I'd been adopted.

After I zipped the suitcase, Gus said, "You're the man of the house now." He used his remaining hand to jab my shoulder.

The blow didn't hurt, but I flinched.

The Bronco had been sold to pay the doctors and the hospital, so Gus took a Greyhound bus from Oregon to Nevada.

Mother drove her minivan to the bus station. I tagged along because I wanted another chance to say goodbye. We drove with the windows rolled down, since the van's air conditioning was busted.

The dusty road was hot enough to fry eggs. Gus's brow was beaded with sweat, but he wore a thick wool shirt, the right sleeve hanging below his stump.

Mother pulled into the parking lot. Clouds were rolling in, and some of the heat had abated. A breeze carried the scent of freshly cut alfalfa. Before I could grab the suitcase, Gus took it and said, "Bye, Mother. Bye, Pete."

It was a relief to see Gus smiling for the first time since the accident. I hugged him and said, "Goodbye."

The bus had just pulled away when Mother said she needed to use the restroom.

Cars and trucks whizzed past the parking lot. Many were marked with dents and rust. Small farms in the area were going bust, and it wasn't any easier to make a living at the mill.

A flapping noise made me look up. I raised my hand to shield my eyes from the sun's glare.

"You are a worm," the raven said. "Slither away, or I shall swallow your eyes."

I said, "We're sorry! Please, don't hurt me!"

The bald bird cocked its head. Flecks of gold gleamed in its inky irises. "Prove your fealty."

I knelt on the dusty asphalt, trembling. "What do you want?"

Perhaps it was my imagination, but the flesh around the corners of the raven's beak seemed to curve in a smile. The creature said, "Can you cook?"

4

Each morning before I walked to school, I placed a plate of sliced sirloin on the porch. Very rare, just the outside seared. The raven's gullet was fuller than mine, but its appetite was never satisfied.

By the time I had my thirteenth birthday, the creature's rude taunts had ceased, but incessant demands for finer cuts of meat strained my mother's budget and drove her to consult with a soothsayer, a beautician in Ashland who could predict the future.

"Are you sure that's a good idea?" I said.

Mother nodded. "God helps those who help themselves."

It was Sunday, and the hair salon was closed, but the cotton candy pink room reeked of peroxide and ammonia. The woman who answered the door had the most amazing hair I'd ever seen. It was teased in a high beehive, and the color was pale pink. She wore a pink and black polka dotted sundress and black stiletto heels.

Mother handed her a basket of eggs.

Instead of looking in a crystal ball, the beautician stared at the dregs in a teacup, reading the leaves. She said, "Consume the bald bird's flesh, and the curse will be broken."

Mother said, "The whole bird?"

The fortune teller said, "Just the body. Burn the head, tail, and feet."

▦

Poison would've tainted the meat, so I dissolved a sleeping pill in marinade and drizzled it over filet mignon.

Mother offered to kill the raven, but I insisted that she spend the day in town because my conscience tormented me—if I hadn't thrown the first rock, would Gus have become an amputee?

Unconscious, the raven looked pitiful, beak gaping open. My hand shook when I lifted the cleaver.

The fried breast meat was tender, but the first gamy bite caught in my throat. Straining to breathe, I clutched my neck, nails clawing into my own flesh.

My vision swam with hallucinations of maggots hatching in my coffin, a featherless raven soaring above the grave.

I slammed my belly into the back of a chair. Masticated meat flew from my mouth and landed on the table.

When I'd quit crying, I picked up the glob and ate it, then swallowed flesh from the raven's thigh.

I'd never felt such intense nausea. I dropped the fork. Vomit surged up my throat.

When my stomach emptied, the spasms didn't stop.

Tears ran down my cheeks. My mouth opened wider, but instead of screaming, I shrieked like a raven: *caw!*

I burned the raven's corpse in the backyard. The smoke was black and smelled like despair.

Mother returned in a bright mood, full of gossip and fresh-pressed apple cider. Her joviality turned to horror when she saw the scratches on my throat and heard my desperate *caw, caw, caw!*

The pediatrician's office was about to close, so Mother drove as fast as the minivan would go. She skidded to a stop in the parking lot, nearly hitting a parked car.

After checking my pulse and listening to my chest with his stethoscope, the doctor asked Mother to repeat the story about the raven.

At first he seemed skeptical, but Mother insisted that the bird could speak.

The doctor patted my shoulder. "You've been through quite an ordeal."

Caw, I answered.

He wrote a prescription for an antidepressant. "Don't fret. Your voice will return when you're less stressed."

Mother said, "Can't you do something else to help him?"

He opened a drawer, pulled out a notebook, and handed it to me. "Write about your feelings. Boys who express themselves rationally are less likely to become overwrought."

Mother and the doctor had a private conversation in the hallway outside the examination room while I was getting dressed. The clinic's walls were thin. I heard the doctor say, "Homosexuality."

On the way home, Mother stopped for ice cream. She bought me a hot fudge sundae topped with whipped cream, but my stomach was so queasy I only ate two bites.

Twelve days later, I still could only *caw*. I'd been taking the antidepressant, and I watched a video to learn how to meditate. Practicing breathing exercises made me feel more relaxed, but it didn't get rid of the knot in my stomach. It was as if the raven's flesh was still inside me, festering.

Storm clouds blackened the sky, churning with the promise of lightning. Despite the gloomy weather, I sat on the porch, sketching in my notebook. Drawing landscapes helped me to think less about my inability to speak.

Rain began pelting the earth. I was about to go inside when I saw the sheriff's SUV driving towards our house. I knew something terrible had happened. He never made social calls.

He asked my mother to sit down and gripped her hand.

Color washed from her face. She said, "What's happened?"

Gus's body was found on the shore of Lake Tahoe. He'd been strangled. There were black feathers shoved down his throat.

3β

The night I learned that my brother had been murdered, I began losing my hair.

Mother was convinced that the wicked bird had cursed me, but we sought a second opinion from an internist in Medford.

"Alopecia," the new doctor said.

By the time my head was bald, glossy black feathers were growing from my arms and legs: at first, only a sprinkling of plumage. Mother helped me to pluck the feathers before school.

We tried medications prescribed by doctors, and Mother ordered herbal treatments and ointments from the Internet, but they didn't work.

The soothsayer cast a healing spell, but it didn't counteract the curse.

As fall became winter, the feathers multiplied. Each time a new quill sprouted, my skin itched so much that I had to wear mittens indoors so I wouldn't scratch.

Heavy sweaters hid most of the plumage, but quills poked through the wool. My friends defended me, but the class clown was relentless in his teasing.

The principal called me a "disruptive influence," and ordered me to leave school.

Mother was enraged that I'd been banished, but I insisted on staying home.

Eventually, feathers covered my palms, making it impossible for me to milk the cow and do my other chores.

Unable to keep up the farm, Mother had to sell. We moved into a cottage on the outskirts of town. After Mother explained that she wanted to live a quiet life, the neighbors rarely visited.

Five months later, I woke up with a tail, and my toenails had become claws.

The only positive thing about the metamorphosis was that Mother started buying me dresses. My tail was so wide I couldn't wear pants.

Mother tried to keep my transformation a secret, but the postman was a terrible gossip.

R

Years passed slowly when you lived like a hermit, but developing my artistic skills kept me from growing maudlin. I'd progressed from making sketches to painting with watercolors, acrylics, and oils.

Mother sold my paintings through a local gallery. Income from the art, plus Mother's job at the hardware store, brought in enough money for us to live comfortably.

Mother made spinach lasagna and a lemon cake to celebrate my twenty-first birthday. Ever since I'd killed the raven, the smell of meat made me nauseous. I couldn't eat poultry, beef, lamb, or pork without vomiting.

I was stoop-shouldered and had the wrinkled face of a seventy-year-old. There was no hair on my noggin. My eyelashes and eyebrows were gone.

Every year, my plumage had thickened. I'd plucked, shaved, waxed, even tried electrolysis, but feathers grew back overnight.

The seasons changed, leaves morphed from green to gold and burgundy, snow fell, crocus blossoms poked from newly thawed ground, but my days were always the same. I stood in the living room beside my easel, painting landscapes. It was hard to pretend that I didn't hear children scampering back and forth on our cottage's porch.

Usually, I didn't confront them, but I finally chased a particularly bratty kid into the driveway. I didn't shout, because I wouldn't give him the satisfaction of hearing me *caw*, but he must've told his parents about the "freak" wearing the dress, because people started picketing outside the house.

Mother and I packed our things and left town in the middle of the night. After spending a couple of nights in cheap roadside motels, Mother rented a cottage in Eastern Oregon.

During sunset, the rocky cliffs in the distance glowed in an ethereal kaleidoscope. Since we lived at the end of a lane, with no neighbors nearby, I'd moved my easel to the porch.

The screen door *creaked* as it opened. "What're you painting?" Mother said.

"Wallowa Lake and the ridges in the distance." I touched my brush to the top of a peak, creating a snowdrift.

"What's that beside the trees? A woman?"

I glanced where she pointed. Sure enough, there was a hazy figure outlined in a thin wash of grey paint. It was more of a sketch than a fully-developed person, but it did look like a woman. She wore a dress and a hat. "I don't remember painting her." I frowned.

Mother said, "It's a nice change from your usual landscapes. Adds a bit of mystery." She patted my shoulder. "Don't stay up too late." She walked back into the cottage.

I grabbed the brush that I'd used to paint trees and dipped it into green paint, intending to cover up the figure. When the bristles touched the woman's skirt, my wrist twitched. Pain surged from my hand to my shoulder. Gasping, I dropped the brush on the porch.

The woman's head had turned. Before, she was standing with her face in profile. Now, she was staring at me!

"I'm sorry," I said. My hand trembled, but it was a dull throb, not a sharp pain. I picked up the brush, cleaned it, and dipped it into grey paint.

As I removed the green smudge from the dress, I felt warmth wash over me like a summer breeze, though it was a cool May evening.

A vision flitted through my mind. I saw a winged creature.

My heart beat faster. Inspired, I added more grey paint to the brush and stroked it against the canvas, painting faster than I'd ever painted before. Another hazy figure appeared next to the woman—A dragon.

▽̵

My fanciful paintings sold for higher prices than my previous canvases.

Visions came to me while I was awake and in dreams; not just dragons, bizarre creatures that danced and floated through light beams and mist. Mother worried that they might be demons, but I was convinced that they were angels.

The beauty of the desert was inspiring, and my imagination flourished, but not all of my visions were joyous.

On the anniversary of my brother's death, I always dreamt of the bald raven, perched on Gus's shoulder. The bird's voice resonated like a bell; my brother sounded gruffer than I remembered. Together, they chorused, "Toss another stone, your arm shall be shorn."

♙

Magic potions weren't supposed to be real, but sometimes truth really was stranger than fiction.

At 9:37 AM on a Saturday, the day before the summer solstice, I met someone who looked like she belonged in a fairy tale.

A petite lady I'd never seen before stood on the front porch. She'd appeared out of nowhere. I hadn't heard footsteps on the gravel path, and there was no car parked in the driveway.

She rang the doorbell—again, and again, and again, and again.

Caw, I called to Mother.

I peered through a gap in the curtains.

The visitor was so short that I couldn't see her face. Her hat resembled a bird's nest. Not a small nest for a robin, a cone shape bigger than a skillet made from twigs, moss, clumps of lint, and silver filaments that looked like tinsel stolen from a Christmas tree.

She rapped on the door. "Pete, I have a present for you. Please, open the door."

I heard the kitchen faucet turn off. Mother walked into the foyer. "Who is it?" she said.

Caw. I shrugged my shoulders.

The teakettle whistled.

I hurried to the kitchen. Since our house was small, I could hear their voices.

The visitor said, "I have a special delivery for your son."

Mother said, "I'll take it."

"The gift must be delivered personally."

"My son's not feeling well."

"He'll feel a lot better after he receives his gift."

"Ma'am. Stop!" Mother shouted.

I heard a scuffle, a screech, and the patter of little feet skittering towards the kitchen. Heavier footfalls thudded in pursuit.

There was nowhere to hide except for the broom closet. I yanked open the door. The closet was so small, my tail pressed against the wall. In my haste, I knocked over the mop, which struck a shelf of cleaning supplies. A bottle tumbled to the linoleum. The cap came off, and lemon-scented fluid splashed my ankles. I pressed my lips together, but couldn't stifle a sneeze.

"How dare you!" Mother said. Her voice sounded closer.

The lady said, "I'm sorry for the intrusion, but this is an urgent matter."

The closet door swung open.

The lady said, "Pete, I brought you a cake." She backed away from the closet. Her lips parted in a smile. She had two prominent buckteeth, like a rabbit. "I'm Drucilla Duncan, Righter of Wrongs. You can call me Dru."

My knees shook. This had to be a sick joke.

Mother said, "Leave, now!"

"After he eats his cake," Dru said. She set the pink package she'd been holding on the countertop. She wasn't much taller than four feet, but her hands were as large as catcher's mitts.

Mother's face turned red. "Out!" Mother took a step, as if she was about to lunge.

Dru snapped her fingers.

Mother froze mid-motion, one foot off the floor, her hands outstretched.

Caw! I screeched.

Dru said, "Don't worry, your mother will be fine. I'll let her move after you eat the cake." She gave me another toothy smile. "Please, come out of the closet. I won't hurt you."

Something propelled me forward. I took one step, then another, dragging my claws across the floor.

Dru lifted the lid from the box. Golden light spilled into the kitchen.

I heard a *pop*. The light dissipated.

She said, "Your cake is ready."

The cake was tiny, the size of a quail's egg, and had an oblong shape. The color of the icing kept shifting. First it was pink, then gold, then a shimmery purple.

Dru removed one of her white gloves. Her hand was covered in thick grey fur, like an animal's paw.

She said, "Hold still," and rubbed the paw against my chin.

Soothing warmth spread down my neck to my belly. Suddenly, I was ravenous.

She said, "Open your mouth."

My lips parted.

"Chew thoroughly. Don't swallow until I say."

It was like biting into whipped cream, except there were crunchy bits.

"Keep chewing," she said.

Flavors rolled across my tongue. Honey, and something spicy. No, not spicy. Earthy. A mushroom? No, that wasn't right, either. Lavender?

My molars ground into a particularly hard morsel. Regret? How could regret have a flavor and a scent?

The goo in my mouth stiffened and became sticky nougat. The flavor shifted, becoming sour. Each chew took more effort. I began to sweat. The heat in my belly spread to my knees. I smelled burning feathers, but my skin didn't feel like it was being singed. When I looked down, my plumage had not disappeared.

Dru's eyes gleamed. The irises changed from deep blue to pale turquoise. She said, "Close your eyes and make a wish. Now, swallow."

The masticated cake felt like a fiery coal as it slid down my throat. Pain made me collapse and writhe on the floor.

Invisible ropes lashed to my wrists and ankles, pulling, stretching my bones.

The last thing I remembered was hearing a shrill scream burst from my mouth. Not a *caw*; a woman's voice.

aaa

When I regained consciousness, my feathers were gone, and my back wasn't hunched. Those weren't the only changes. I'd grown five inches, and instead of having a flat chest, I had breasts. My nipples didn't just stick out. I had voluptuous curves.

Mother pulled me towards the hallway mirror.

My face looked like it had traveled through a time machine. Instead of being old and haggard, I had a smooth, glowing complexion. The hair on my head had regrown, but it wasn't short and auburn; a thick lavender mane flowed halfway down my back.

Dru grasped my hand. "Sit down, and I'll tell you a story."

When we were seated on the living room sofa, Dru said, "You had to die, so you could live again."

"I'm dead?" I gasped. My chest felt so tight I could barely breathe.

"Not dead, reincarnated." Dru smiled.

Mother said, "What've you done to my son?"

Dru said, "Magic can be unpredictable. Sometimes there's a glitch."

Mother said, "A glitch! He looks like a woman!"

Dru said, "We can try again. Shall we, Pete? Shall I fetch another cake?"

A tear trickled down my cheek. I touched my new hair. It was silky, and lavender was my favorite color.

Mother and I had to move again. Our neighbors would've asked too many questions.

Dru helped us to rent an apartment in Portland. It was a small, two-bedroom unit on the top floor of a triplex, but we didn't need a lot of space, and the building was a Victorian, on a quiet street. From the turret window, you could see Mount Hood.

We didn't bring many of our old belongings, and I left my old name behind, too. I'd never liked being called Pete, or being a boy. Madeline was a better fit for my personality.

Adjusting to my new body was easier than I expected, but learning about magic was arduous work. Fortunately, Dru was patient, and an excellent teacher.

The pot on the stove bubbled as steam rose towards the ceiling.

"Stir it again," Dru said. "Not so fast, gently. Don't whip the nougat until the scales melt."

"Sorry," I said. "Is this the right speed?"

She nodded, and used a handkerchief to dab sweat from my forehead.

I'd been toiling over the hot stove for nearly three hours, but I didn't complain. It was the first time Dru had allowed me to help her make icing. Apprentices weren't permitted to assist with baking cakes.

The dragon peeled another scale from his tail. When the moon wasn't full, Ferdinand was the size of a housecat and looked like an ordinary iguana lizard, except for his opposable thumbs.

Dru dropped the scale into the pot, and I stirred again.

The mixture *hissed*, and the liquid changed color, becoming a darker shade of pink as the scale melted, which was strange, since Ferdinand's scales were green.

My first batch of icing was a flop. So was the second batch, and the third, fourth, fifth, and sixth. Perhaps I'd never master the culinary arts, but Dru let me help with deliveries.

Maybe I could've had a career as a fashion model, but doing good deeds was much more satisfying. People weren't always happy to see me, but I never left until I'd accomplished my mission.

I shifted the pink package to my left hand and pressed the doorbell.

A little boy answered.

I said, "Hello, dear. I have a present for your mother.

"Sorrow is sometimes sweetest on the tongue, don't you find?" I ask, refilling your mug as the narrative unravels.

The magpie flutters and lands on top of the microwave, cocking its head at you and staring deeply in a way that makes you itch. Your lips purse, and your eyes zoom around the room, the breath hitching in your chest for a minute.

"What... what's happening?" you ask.

"You're witnessing," I say simply. "Martyr to the miseries of a bound and burdened muse."

"What was in that tea?"

"I told you," I say, sipping my own. "Rosehips, licorice, and coriander. And alright, you caught me—I snuck in some marshmallow root." Setting the mug on the table, I again sit down across from you, and the coin is back in my hand, dancing along my knuckles, looking out at you with its blind eye and sucking you down, down, down into the stamped iris.

"You're here, with me, and you've paid a lovely fee to toss lovely bones on a lovely night with a lonely lover, and you're looking at me, and I'm looking at you... I'm speaking, and I'm telling, and I'm taking you with me with each telling, and you can't look away, and you can't help being looked at by me as I take us down again, because after all, everyone wants to be..."

SEEN

Ju Collins

Jamie's eyes snapped open, and the blurry room started to slowly come into focus. Their back was against a blank wall, which they leaned on heavily for support. Alarm began to rise thick in their throat, bubbling like acid, because the room did not make sense. A dim and blinking fluorescent light hung loosely from the centre of the ceiling, barely illuminating the corners of the room. Nothing they saw was familiar. A sterile environment met every glance; white walls with white trim and no windows or decoration, just one solid metal door in the far right corner. *What kind of room doesn't even have so much as a cheap print taped to the wall?* Jamie thought to themselves, trying to quell the fear hidden in their confusion. Swallowing hard to keep the panic at bay, they desperately tried to find any semblance of safety or comfort in the strange room.

Before a shred of certainty could be found, the metal door started to screech. A high-pitched, metal-on-metal sound bombarded them, forcing Jamie to jam their hands over their ears and screw their eyes shut. Then as suddenly as it started, there was complete silence again. Something had changed, Jamie could feel the difference in the air, a different smell, a different feeling. Slowly and cautiously, they lowered their hands to their sides, but somehow they couldn't find the courage to open their eyes quite yet. A slight movement of air brushed past their right hand, then their left, accompanied by a distinct pain at each wrist. A dead cold feeling spread across them from fingertip to toenail. Out of pure animal instinct, they jolted forward in hopes of evading whatever was near them, and possibly reaching the door to escape—though, thinking on it now, Jamie couldn't recall seeing a handle on this side of the door. Expecting to propel their body forward, feeling the air move past them, they were instead met with great resistance and irritating pain at their wrists, and now, ankles. Jamie finally steeled their nerves enough to look around, but first at themselves. There weren't any visible restraints, as they suspected, but their wrists and ankles seemed fused to the wall in an awkward, inhumane way, twisting their limbs at odd angles in order to hold them flat against it. Jamie frantically tried to break free, but the more they struggled, the more the wall ate into their skin in response. Properly freaked out by now, their eyes searched wildly for answers, anything at all that could explain what was happening, or why.

They quickly realized they were no longer alone. Someone well-dressed, but otherwise unremarkable, stood ramrod straight in the middle of the room, staring directly at Jamie with an uneven smirk on their face.

"Welcome, Jamie. You probably have some questions for me, but unfortunately today is not about answers," the stranger said with calm confidence. "Today is all about you." They moved from the centre of the room to the right side, leaning against the wall casually, their feet crossed.

"What do you mean? Why am I here, and how did I get here?" Jamie began, their mind quickly unraveling in the strangeness of it all.

"Ah, ah, ah. See? Questions demanding answers, that's not going to get you anywhere." The stranger moved a little closer, but still maintained the laid-back demeanor. "Oh, I do have one answer for you." They moved closer again, only about four feet away now. "The restraints are customary; it's a safety precaution, you see? There's no way to know what someone might do…"

They started to get lost in their own thoughts, but then their eyes quickly snapped back to Jamie and locked onto their own. "Let's get down to business. You probably want to get back to your busy day, and I have a long list of other… *clients* I need to attend to—So tell me Jamie: what is your desire?"

Jamie became mute with surprise.

"What do you mean? My desire about what?"

They thought their best chance of ever getting out of this, if it was at all possible, was to acquiesce until a better plan became clear.

"Well, folks end up here with me for a reason. When a certain amount of discomfort and pain is noticed, I step in. I'm really here to help you, although I admit this really is a thankless job.". They looked down at their nails, clean and polished but unusually long, then looked up again. "You have a desire that makes the pain lessen, and if you tell me, I can make it happen. It's that simple." The stranger smiled, but it felt like a trap, the face of a predator before it's been detected.

"Here, as an act of good faith, and to get the ball rolling…" They snapped their fingers and the cuffs withdrew immediately from Jamie's wrists. They ached so badly, and the release was a wave of relief.

Jamie rubbed each wrist to get the blood flowing again, and then looked up at the stranger. "Thanks, I guess. So, what, you're like a genie for fucked up people? I'm sorry, but that seems completely made up."

"I won't take offense to that. You'll see." They moved across the room and dug into their left pocket, pulling out an extraordinarily shiny silver coin. They gave it a maniacal spin between their fingers, even spinning it in place on top of their pointer. "You can call me Ash, by the way, not that you asked *that* question." Still spinning the coin they said, "My clients sometimes find it easier to decipher their desires with the help of this." Ash raised an eyebrow and then positioned the coin on top of their thumbnail. They flipped their it quickly outward and the coin flew into the air, shining brilliantly with every spin. Jamie barely had the chance to reach out as it fell directly into the centre of their palm, as if there were a magnet hidden there. The coin was almost too hot to hold, making them shiver, realizing only now how cold the room actually was. Upon brief inspection, the silver coin looked blank. Jamie thought it was awfully odd to offer someone a blank coin, so they flipped it a few times in their palm to see if there was any other significance. A pattern of shimmers appeared on the wall as it turned. Jamie looked closely and noticed it was now quite captivating and descriptive. The first side had a beautifully etched eye, showing incredible detail in the iris, eyelids and eyelashes. It was clearly a human eye, and it was truly the only familiar thing Jamie had seen since first opening their own in this place.

They flipped it over to examine the other side. This side was similar, but not the same. First of all, this eye was not human. It still had the incredible detail and mesmerizing etching as the first side, but it didn't evoke comfort. The iris was thin and slanted at a cruel angle, making it seem angry. Without context, it's hard to imagine an eye conveying anger or disgust, but this one did it effortlessly. Looking directly at it made Jamie want to shrink away in fear of being in its view. The skin around the white was scaly and rough, textured upon the metal. There were no eyelashes, but Jamie could see the beginning of an outline of something that just barely made it on the coin before the edge. It seemed like bone, or maybe a tooth? No, a tooth didn't make sense, not near an eye. The realization crept in slowly, igniting chills up and down their spine. A horn. It was the beginning of a horn. What kind of creature was this? What kind of coin was this? Before the onslaught of questions could continue, Ash cleared their throat and interrupted them.

"So. What do you think? Has anything caught your eye?" Ash smirked, then frowned quickly; "It doesn't usually take this long." Ash looked down at their wrist, as if this appointment was running late and it was annoying them, but they weren't wearing a watch that Jamie could see.

"I'm not sure what to make of all this. This coin has two really weird, similar sides. Every coin that I've ever seen has two drastically different ones. What's the meaning of the eyes?" Jamie pondered aloud..

"Ah, I see. That's a common one, honestly." Ash moved even closer this time, within arm's of reach of Jamie. They could smell something distinct, like something burnt beyond recognition of what it once was. *It's not quite burnt toast*, Jamie thought, but being able to blame this fever dream on a stroke seems like the best case scenario at this point.

"Each coin reflects a desire back to the inquirer. It helps clear things up on my end, as well.". Ash took the coin from Jamie's hand frighteningly fast, almost imperceptible until it had already happened. "Mhm, there are always two sides to everything, isn't there Jamie? Even if they might seem similar, they certainly are not." They flicked the coin with their thumb once more and it landed squarely and easily into Jamie's shirt pocket. "For safe keeping." Ash winked. For the first time Jamie realized that part of the uneasiness they felt was because Ash had not blinked once since Jamie first saw them.

"What time is it? How long have I even been here?" Jamie blurted out, unable to contain the panicked questions Ash had already warned them about.

"Time is just perception, Jamie. It only exists within you, not outside of you. Perhaps you've been here a few minutes, maybe a few hours. Hell, maybe it's been a few days? Who is to say, the passing of time is a different department, so to speak." Ash turned and briskly walked toward the metal door, stopping and twirling on the ball of their foot to face Jamie once again. "So tell me quickly, what is your desire?" Ash stared at Jamie, not blinking.

Jamie thought on the changing of the coin, and on one particular desire that had been burning through their guts since childhood. It suddenly lit up in their brain like a neon sign, like someone had just flicked the switch.

"To be seen." Jamie said.

Ash smiled without showing teeth, "Good. That's something I can work with."

"I mean really being seen for who I really am. Outside and in between gender, without gender. It's painful to feel like you just fall between the cracks of society, and that's exactly where everyone wants you to stay. Being swiped away like an uninvited bug at the picnic called life. I don't want to live like that anymore." Jamie started to well up, but breathed deeply and found a small spark of excitement that Ash might really be able to help. Nothing had ever been able to quell this deep unsettling in Jamie since they were a little kid, maybe this was finally their chance. To be fair, no one had ever really offered to help in any significant way before.

Ash placed a hand on the metal door. A low sizzling sound rang through Jamie's ears.

"I understand completely. You'll find I follow directions very well," Ash said, and moved the hand on the door quickly backward. The door swung open with a quick, sharp screech and remained open long enough for Jamie to see Ash step out. Their jaw slacked open at the sight of it. Ash stepped out into complete emptiness. If Jamie could even begin to process what they had seen, it seemed as if there was nothing at all outside this room. Ash began to simply disappear inch by inch as they passed through the doorframe. The empty, dark space outside the door looked like it had mass, a smooth and wavy textured cloth that simply swallowed everything it touched. Jamie no longer wanted to ever pass through that door.

"So, when—" Jamie frantically began, but was cut off mid-sentence by complete and utter darkness as the metal door clanged shut. The blackness closed in on them, holding every part of them, caressing their senses into dullness. Although they couldn't see if they tried, they felt their eyes being forced closed. Impossibly heavy, impossible to resist. Once they closed for good, Jamie started to feel their consciousness slipping away. It was like the feeling of being trapped between wakefulness and sleep, the feeling of being haunted by the old hag, never waking, just *enduring*. It felt like being trapped in the expansive blanket of emptiness Jamie imagined was outside the metal door. Nothing and everything at the same time. The darkness swallowed Jamie, and they let it. They could no longer feel the wall behind them, the coldness of the room on their skin, or the restraint of their ankles. The only sensation was the burning of the coin through their shirt and into their chest. Their last words to Ash exploded through the darkness to the forefront of their thoughts like a red hot coal. *I don't want to live like this anymore.* The sizzling noise started again, first low and constant, then louder and louder, deafening and erratic like TV static on maximum volume. "No!" Jamie screamed, as the realization of their mistake dawned on them. Their own screaming voice filled their ears for only a second before the air was robbed from their throat—

—Then silence.

X

That silence lingers in the air for a moment, and then the coin disappears again with a flash.

You want to ask what really happened, want to know where they went when they weren't themself anymore… but you understand the contract, and know that to ask a question like that would be tantamount to a violation, almost an assault. You keep your own counsel, troubled, and I stroke the magpie under the chin as they hop over onto my arm, Deedee eyeing them with suspicion.

It feels like you're bobbing for apples, gasping for air as the nondescript room once again becomes my humble abode, and you find your own wrists free to move, to be touched with your fingers in supplication.

"Another from the trove, I think…" I say, returning to the shelf, eyes striding over the spines in a familiar ritual, choosing, deciding, arranging the same way that the musicians who played tonight place their notes before and after one another.

A sneaky little volume almost escapes my notice, a lichenous little villain, thin and lean and mean, and my fingers snatch it before it can escape. As I pull it from the shelf, the perfume in the cabin changes from floral to putrid standing water, algae nipping at fish guts, the sharp tingle and tang of pinesap and poison.

"This one almost escaped my notice," I say. "Tricky bastard. Hard to pin down, even as it follows you, peering out from the cracks in the shadows of your life… Turn, turn, turn at the right time, and you just might catch a glimpse of the…"

MOSS WITCH OF THE CASCADE MOUNTAINS

Mave Goren

Idunn-Rapids was run by witches. A small blip of a Western Washington town, consisting of two streets, a park, and antique stores piled wall to wall with useless junk. Stores shuttered early. Some remained shuttered for years. The characteristic Pacific Northwestern decay crept around every inch of the county like shards of broken glass. I'll never forget those foggy nights, when I left the city limits, walking down the road to the dispensary perched atop the highway like a vulture. Rain would soak my dress, making my hair stick to my shoulders like a whip from a soggy towel.

The only reason why you would want to visit I-Rapids is if you have an interest in cryptids. Those strange creatures, the liminal walkers between truth and myth, the American imagination has long been captivated by the fringes of zoology. On the city limits, right by the field of the old Arseth Farmhouse, I-rapids saw its very own cryptid for the first time.

On a moonlit night in the late 70s, Howard Arseth and Will Gunmir went for a walk. The two farmers had been living together since their respective families had died, consolidating resources and trying their best to support each other. In the fall, a wind crept up. It was poor weather for harvesting. Will and Howard walked along that patch of farmland they called their own. Tilled soil snaked its way into a massive clearing. There were no crops to harvest. On a hill, their farmhouse watched like an overbearing parent. The two men made their way around the soil, hugging the massive pine trees that walled them off from the rest of the pacific northwest.

The sky was a violent shade of purple. On nights like that, the clouds were three-dimensional, surrounding the mountainous

landscape like eyeless angels. Will walked like he had somewhere to go, always skirting and walking ahead Howard. He wanted to take a walk to make sure the crops were ok. Howard slouched his way forward, his long graying hair reaching over the shoulders of his overalls.

"Sure is nice out tonight," Howard said.

"You call it nice," Said Will, "But which one of us spent the night at his sewing machine, and which one of us was toiling in the fields?"

"I'm sorry."

"Ain't no sorry about it. Come join me in the fields tomorrow or I'm gonna do something that will make you regret the day you were born."

"Empty threats." Said Howard, "We'll all get what's coming to us someday."

The wind cast its cruel spell on the farmlands, nipping at Will and Howard's faces.

Will was shouting over the crackling howls of mother nature: "There's nothing for us here, there's fucking nothing for us here, and you're just making your little fairy dolls." Will's hands reached for Howard's back, clutching onto them like a ravenous lion.

"Don't disrespect the dolls," said Howard, as he clutched Will's shoulders. The two men were ready to die in the October cold.

Over the crackling wind, there came a cackling. An ethereal howl, emanating from the depths of the forest.

"Wait, what was that?" Said Howard,

"Some mutt, no doubt."

"No, I heard it, it's coming from the forest." There was a pallid glow from the mass of moss and trees. Branches intertwined into each other, like a garish patchwork quilt. On the ground was a slurry of moss, mold and fallen trees, their dying ochre returning to the earth from whence it came. Howard and Will tussled themselves into the mulch, and into the forest, nicking themselves with brambles and god knows what. The cackling became louder.

A wiry hand was reaching for Will's shoulder. Howard glanced up; a wiry triangular figure stood in the distance, clad in shadowy, moth-eaten robes. On its head flopped a pointy wide-brimmed hat. Its eyes were glowing-bone-white. #

This is what Howard told the Sheriff when he returned alone that night. A strange figure, immortalized in rough police etchings. The work of a preternatural entity: The Moss Witch of the Cascade Mountains. If I were a different person, I would tell you this was the coolest thing ever, that Washington State had a monopoly on the otherworldly. When you work in your town's only museum, this schtick gets old fast. The Moss Witch's coven is in I-Rapids. She lurks the streets, corridors and backyards.   And it is my job to tell tourists this story every day.

I-Rapids hasn't been seeing much tourism as of late. I opened and closed the museum with my boss Mary, cataloging various items about Western Washington natural history on a daily basis. Afterwards, I went across the park to Pete's Diner, drowning my sorrows in medium rare burgers.

It's expected for every trans girl to go through a goth phase at least once in her transition. Growing up in I-Rapids, my way of rebelling from the spectral stagnation was wearing mint green dresses and fiddling around on my guitar. Yet I can't help but have the Moss Witch wash her gothic aura over me. My past self still haunts these very streets. He's lurking the halls of my old high school, sticking his nose through the aisles of the Safeway, reading just about any sci-fi book he can from the library. I might have missed him on an intellectual level, but I wanted him gone.

QE

I pushed open the chrome door to Pete's diner. If this was your first time on earth, you'd think art-deco diners like these were spaceships, temples, chrome skeletons of felled beasts. I was surrounded by marble floors and velveteen cushions. I walked up to Martha, sitting by the front.

"Evening Martha, is Nathan here today?"

"You betcha, Wren."

"Wonderful," I said, "I can't wait."

"Long day at work, huh hon?"

"Oh you know." I said, "It was work."

"Sure is, dear."

Pete's diner never ran out of Elvis songs to play. I can't help but fall in love with them; they remind me of a past that never was. I checked the books in our gift shop, believe me; I-Rapids was never an idyllic suburb in the 50s. There were no white picket fences, no malt shops and skate rinks, no families with two and a half children, no. Instead I-Rapids was dying a slow death, businesses came and went, mostly went.

I mulled over the menu even though I was just getting the cheeseburger. There are times when I think of myself as a masochist due to my propensity for greasy food. Nathan, I was sure, was tired of me telling the same story about the time I got sick in high school. The janitor spent all day cleaning up my vomit. When my mind went back to high school I always thought about vomit. For now, I brushed the thoughts of effluvia aside; I beckoned towards Nathan, ready for a meal.

Nathan was wearing an apron over a shirt with one of his favorite bands, Gorebarian of Hyperborea in a baroque, spiky

logo. It wasn't the easiest thing to read, but then again, neither was Nathan. He shuffled over to where I am, the Elvis playing in the background swelled to its most romantic. "What can I get you, Wren?"

"You know me, Nathan. I'll have the usual."

"One *boigah* coming up." Nathan put on one of his patented "silly voices" this time of a surly New York City burger chef. "How've you been, Nathan?" I said. "Can't say I've had fun at the museum."

"Well I can't say much has happened to me other than flipping burgers."

"I can't say anything else has happened to me except talking to tourists about witches." I said.

"These things happen," Nathan said in a surly receptionist voice, "but, there was something I wanted to tell you about. I get off early tomorrow, can we link at 6?"

"Sure, I'm always down to hang with my main man Nathan," I said,

"Well this is a little more important than that. I've… uh… been having issues."

"Issues, huh? What kind?"

"I'll tell you tomorrow, okay? I gotta get your burger under way." Nathan disappeared into the gloom of the kitchen, humming bleepy video game soundtracks to himself. I flipped open my phone, checking to see if social media would be an amusing little distraction before my meal. There were three of us back then, Kate, Nathan and yours truly. We liked to smoke weed, listen to Nirvana and chill behind the old Arseth Farmhouse. Time passed and I came out as a woman. A couple of years later Kate comes out too, and an electronic musician to boot. Then she moved to Seattle and I lost contact with her. Was it now Nathan's turn? I never thought Kate was an obvious case. Nathan wasn't much different. Yeah, he's a scruffy guy with knowledge of obscure-ass heavy metal bands and dry surrealist comedy, but we don't assume every nerdy autistic boy grows up to be a beautiful woman, do we? I wouldn't have ruled it out, but the last thing I wanted was teaching another baby trans how to girl.

I scrolled on my phone, entering an endless rabbit hole of exactly why I hate social media. The modern internet has a tendency to break everything into microlabels of microlabels.

This is why you see people calling themselves Anarcho-Monarchists or Catholic Leninists. The trans community is no exception. I scrolled past posts about puppygirls, mutuals kissing each other, gloating about their success, inane political discourse. Kill me now.

Nathan wheeled out my burger with an extra pickle. Sometimes I feel as if I am the sole person responsible for propping up Pete's Diner from its inevitable ruin. No one else is in the diner, just me, the wait staff and the cooks. "Thank you for your service." I said,

"My pleasure, Wren."

"Anytime fam. Just so you know, you can tell me about anything you have your mind on, okay?"

"I told you," he said, imitating a mafioso, "We'll link tomorrow. But enjoy your burger, I insist."

I pause mid-eating, my mouth full of ground beef. "Too late, Nathan."

⅄

I tipped Nathan extra well and left the diner, my belly full of greasy comfort food. Downtown I-Rapids was bathed in a cold blackness. It's been getting darker as of late. Fog crept across the street. The trees in the park reached out like long fingers, the streets strewn with dead leaves. In the chrome exterior of the diner, I scrounged for a preroll in my purse and set it ablaze. Smoke rose into the cold Cascadian sky like a censer to the heavens. There's nothing quite like smoking weed after a good meal. When I was done, I tossed it on the ground where it found its home among the ochre mush of leaves and cigarette butts. I began my walk back to my Dad's place.

⍓

Our house was on a hill, at the far end of town. All of I-Rapids is walkable, even the natural areas which lurk in the distance. My hands planted in my dress pockets, I shuffled through the piles and piles of leaves, my mind buzzing with the heady rush of THC.

As I continued strolling down the street, there was a little trudge of footsteps. They were coming right behind me. Who in their right minds would be out this late in I-Rapids? I continued walking, my feet were killing me. The wind bit at my clothes, my hands became raw and numb.

The clomping started again.

I turned my entire body around.

Nothing was there.

I might have had too much weed, my body seized with sharp

needles, congealing in my stomach like a vat of blood. Could it be that my mind was playing tricks on me? No, I was sure I'd have to smoke an absurd amount for that. Nothing was there, just powerlines, black street lamps and dying trees. It meant a lot to me that I was close to my house, it was just a little ways to go. *Just a little ways to go.*

The footsteps grew louder, a thick thumping against mushy leaves. My heart was beating so loud, it could have burst right from my chest. I bolted. My purse was hitting my dress as I dashed towards my Dad's house. I was almost there.

At last, I began the climb up the hill. Washington State was so hilly, you could swear it was built on graves of sleeping gods. I heaved my body upwards. Dad's house lurked at the very top. I could see its scarlet awning, it was so close. The thumping didn't cease. I didn't turn my head around, I had no idea *what* I would see, a human, an eldritch god, the Moss Witch? I didn't want it to touch me.

I was heaving from exhaustion the time I made it to the top of the hill. I ran up to the front porch, reaching for my key. I turned the knob and scurried inside. I slammed the door shut. I was sure Dad would hear my commotion, but he would be glad to know I was safe. I scrambled up the hardwood steps and into my room, locking my door. I collapsed in my bed, staring at the ceiling.

My room was a small beige shoebox. Posters from the Museum of Natural History flooded the walls. I was glad to be back in a room filled with thrushes and finches, rushes of adrenaline and flinches of nerves. I had more work tomorrow; a student group was visiting. I couldn't wait to do the same damn routine over again, and maybe sort through documents no one cares about, or touch up a taxidermied wolverine for good measure.

I got up from my bed, reaching for my estradiol. All my friends online swore by injections, but the clinic I went to only would give me estradiol pills. When you've been on HRT for so long, you start to wish it could work its magic as soon as possible, and maybe give you free FFS and a romantic spaghetti dinner while you wait. The little teal tablets dissolved under my tongue. My mind was a TV, tuned to a dead channel. I set the alarm and collapsed back into my bed, hoping I'd wake up in time.

ᚦ

I made it to the museum on the other side of town 5 minutes before it would open. These days, only me and Mary run the whole thing. It's a little log shack, bearing a striking resemblance to the log cabins the old Swedish settlers would build. If I were younger I'd have thought it was rustic and cute; now I took account of how many termites lived in these walls. I reached in my purse for my key, opening the door. Mary wasn't here, *oh joy*. Little glass cases filled with natural bric-a-brac were lit by the pale light of sun which inched its way through the windows. I turned on the lights, and moved to the back of the museum, where I signed in by paper. Mary wasn't here yet. For now it was a One-Wren-Show.

I still couldn't shake off that feeling I had last night. Something was following me. When I was hauling thick cardboard boxes out of the way so that I could make room for walking in the museum, some creature scurried in the furthest shadowy corners. Twigs snapped outside, a rustle for a moment, and then complete silence. Sweat dripped down my brow. *Just grin and bear it, Wren.*

ᛟ

It was 11:00 in the morning and Mary hadn't shown up yet. I had to make sure the museum was in its utmost condition, ducking down to dust cobwebs which amassed on the cases, piling files and archives into the ever-bulging closet. Sooner than later, I had to clean up the Moss Witch room.

As cluttered as a conspiracy theorist's attic, the Moss Witch room was littered with newspaper clippings wall to wall. The police sketch of the Moss Witch was cut, copied and pasted over and over again over the wall. We just needed a cork board with yellow string connecting the Moss Witch to Bigfoot, chemtrails and UFOs and we'd be all set. In the center were little glass cases with farm equipment from the Arseth estate, as well as little dolls made from needles. They had no eyes other than that of sewing needles. No child would have wanted to play with them, unless they enjoyed cuddling pincushions. No, these were poppets, pure and simple. Dolls with a power behind them. A piercing, striking power.

I was dusting the giant model I-Rapids made of the Moss Witch for the state fair when the door squealed open. My conscience told me it was Mary, coming in to help supervise me, but my body froze with terror. At once, I was pricked with needles, by those same needle dolls, eyeless, but with many eyes. Tromping, the sound of flat-soled feet on the hardwood floor and Mary emerges from the gloom.

"Hi Wren," she said.

"Hi Mary, just cleaning up the museum."

"As you should." Mary cleared her throat. She was wearing a little flower dress, not dissimilar from the one I was wearing, but she probably didn't shoplift it from TJ Maxx.

"Listen Wren," She said, "We have a school group coming in today at 2pm. Are you prepared?"

"I'm ready as I'll ever be."

"I'm expecting a little more town spirit."

"Uh, I'm ready."

"Atta boy—sorry, I mean girl."

"It's okay." I said, wishing I was done with the damn conversation.

There were no visitors until 3pm. The time before was spent on my phone, absorbed in the same three apps, waiting for *Something* to happen. I couldn't wait until I was done with work so Nathan could tell me about his (their?) problem. I kept a copy of *Nevada* by Imogen Binnie in my backpack, just in case.

Let me tell you, it was hard to be distracted by your phone and social media when you had a boss in the other room who respected none of your privacy. As soon as I found the right web rabbit hole to go down on, Mary would give me a task.

"Go sort the papers detailing the Arseth House's history." "Sure thing Mary."

"Go catalog this Thrush."

"Sure thing Mary."

"Go send an email to our donors."

"Sure thing Mary." When Mr. Svensson's 9th grade class waltzed in, I was elated. I guided the group of sickly teens through the halls, explaining in as convivial a style as I could. We snaked through the natural history exhibit, they inched behind me, savoring as much of a time they'd have outside of the house. We got to the Moss Witch room. On an average High School visit, the kids would be elated to visit such a spooky and macabre slice of americana, but this time?

"Now we are going to enter the darkest room of the museum," I said, "The Moss Witch room!" I imitated a theremin in a 50s sci-fi movie.

The children had blank faces like antagonists in an old horror movie, but they didn't have blood or corn on their minds, they just wanted to go home and play video games, I was sure of it.

I led them into the room, the children were greeted by conspiracy theory wallpaper and strange folk-art. I dimmed the lights. The fluorescent light bulb hummed its doleful tune.

"On a moonlit night in the 70s," I began, "two farmers were—"

That rustling in the bushes came back. It grew. Somewhere between a maraca and a swarm of bees. It was coming from right behind the window.

"Uh, Miss?" one of the students raised his hand, "are you alright?"

"Yeah!?" I said, rivulets of sweat dripping down my brow. "Does it not look like I am?"

"I'd appreciate it if you kept your tone with the students," Mr. Svensson said.

"What do you mean?" I said, "I am calm, I am."

"I was just wondering," the student said.

I continued the tour. When I continued to speak, I'd hear that little *shuffle-shuffle* sound in the back of my mind, and despite the heat, beads of sweat would drop from my forehead. It was as if I was performing a comedy routine in my underwear, those children could see directly into my soul, I swear.

"Great job as always, Wren," Mary said, her arms crossed, kicking her foot against the wall. "You can clock out now."

I signed out, giving myself a couple of extra hours on the timesheet for good measure. Rushing out the door, I ran across the street, as far from the bushes as possible. Now I was in the park, walking on the little brick pathway towards Pete's diner, ready for Nathan to tell me the truth.

⚐

After dinner, I approached Nathan, eager to hear what was going on.

"Yo, Wren?"

"What's up my guy? Have something to tell me?"

"Yeah, but can we walk a little bit before?"

"Uh, sure."

"Then let's go."

"Ya know," I said, "You can tell me anything that's on your mind. That's what friends are for, right?"

"Just a little bit, then we can talk." No accents this time, that was odd.

We strolled down that street lined with rows of jagged houses, distinct from each other but uniform in their adherence to prosaicism. There was not a peep from either of us, just the tweeting of birds and the blustering wind. The sky above us was a brilliant purple. It was so vast, I could swear that it was going to swallow up me and Nathan at any minute. We kept walking.

Once you start walking around I-Rapids, you realize how spare everything is. The further out you walk, the further houses are spaced apart. It's like the areas of a video game where the screen forgets to load all of its assets. I wouldn't be surprised if the houses were made of nothing but polygons and vector graphics.

"Is now a good time?" I said,

"Just a little further."

It got hillier. As we walked up a steep incline, I wished I didn't order the burger for the 42nd time. My insides will be the death of me. We were ascending the hill like monks in search of enlightenment. In the furthest back, surrounded by dying fields of vast overgrown weeds, we saw that house—the Arseth farmhouse. It blended into the mountains like a set of teeth. Nathan made furtive glances around, even though no one was there.

"Okay," He said, out of breath. "Coast is clear." "I'm all ears!" I said, pointing at my ears.

"Wren, this might sound crazy, but I think you're the only person who can believe me about this."

"I'm listening." *Here it comes.*

"Wren, I've, I've been feeling like I've been hunted. Like there's someone stalking me."

"God." I said, "Same."

Nathan grabbed my shoulder. The chill wind coursed through my body, causing our hairs to stand on end.

"It keeps following me." he said, "in my shadows and in my dreams. I have no earthly idea of *what* it is. Wren… I'm scared."

"M-me too."

We embraced in the autumn night. The Arseth house was seething, glowing with a violent energy. Nathan's tears and whimpers buried themselves in my dress. The Arseth house was peeling apart, its walls shedding and curling like an exoskeleton. It glowered back at me, an icy glance through the icy wind. My heart was pounding a steady 4/4 rhythm, so deep and so hard it could break out of my ribcage at any moment.

"I'm gonna move out," Nathan said, "One of these days I'm

gonna save up and move out. Maybe to Seattle, I don't know. But I can't stay here forever."

"I feel the same damn thing," I said, "so am I."

Together on that cold night, we rotted. The thread of youth in I-Rapids was bound to be severed, Nathan and I would cut the string.

33

Our walk back down the hill was a silent affair. I checked to see if there was anything behind us, following us. It was my imagination, nothing more. And also Nathan's. We got to Nathan's house, which sat just next to the diner.

Two trees stood against it like pillars, or curtains in a theater.

"Wren," he said, "please be safe."

"You too buddy."

I sprinted back home, not wanting to risk the chance of anyone following me or trailing behind me. The night was dark and cold. Clouds scraped through the sky like desire lines. The cracks in the sidewalk swarmed with weeds and mushrooms. I was panting even harder, making my way up the hill on the very opposite end.

On my porch, I panted, grasping for my key in my purse. Turning the lock, I ran upstairs and shut the door to my room. I messaged Nathan, asking if he was alright. I flopped down on my mattress, sinking into every inch of the bed, my body gripped with terror. I was at home in those creases which stretched like gnarled oak, if only because for 8 hours every night I'd leave I-Rapids, entering a dreamless slumber. Nathan's plight never left its grasp from my mind. I turned off the lights, put down my phone, continuing to sink deep into my mattress. Through the window, the mass of branches and pine trees congregated in the autumn night sky like a coven of witches. It was a cloudy night, Washington never reaches sub-thermal levels but each year, it began a process of slowly dying. The sky bleak and rainy, the streets pocked with every imperfection imaginable. Dread

coalesced in my heart, trees will die, and soon enough, so will I.

It took an awful long time for me to fall asleep. My body was tight, rigid like a corpse, as if I downed an adderall as a nightcap. Pale light dripped through the window of my room, and as much as I tried to clamp my eyes shut, I kept staring at the window. A breeze had begun to seep through the cracks, my house far too old and uninsulated to do anything about it. My flesh was tattooed by goosepimples. I tried to rest, to surrender myself to infinity, and I might have been making grounds. I was not operating on logic of the waking world. The shadows in my room grew larger, looming over me like nagging thoughts. I sank deeper into my mattress, pinned in place by hypnagogia. But I stared outside that window, the dreamy vast shadows of cascadian decay growing larger like an uncut weed, an untouched piece of peat moss.

A face, gnarled and wrinkled, was staring back at me. A gnarled face, glowing a light blue the color of bloated corpses in the moonlight, it hovered, like a phantom, its hair whipping onto the sides of my house like tendrils. My heart thudded in its chest blood pumping to every chamber of my veins, tighter than a cage, a clenched fist. I looked out again—darkness there, and nothing more.

I woke from dreams that left me raw, impossible to describe, far too familiar and wrong—the same emotions behind a family dinner that breaks out in argument, the nagging guilt of ages past. I lurched out of bed, and stared at my wiry naked body, too masculine to be described as a woman's, breasts too large, skin too soft, to ever be thought of as a man's again. I walked the same limbo between borders as a town on the side of the road, only stopped for gas. If you're hungry on a road trip and stop at a diner there, you might have a glance at the local newspaper, wondering, *just who lives here, who has lived and died behind these fences, at these schools, in these churches, do they realize that I pay them no heed as I hie to my next destination, for I am the hero in my story, and you are but a nodule in my Campbellian Journey.*

When I grabbed my clothes, I checked the alarm clock. 11:00 AM. Just my luck, I overslept. I force my dress on, and rush downstairs and down a cup of coffee in the kitchen. The black tar seeps down to my gullet, my bleary eyes fogged with the unconsciousness that lies beyond my synapses. I rush out the door and down the hill and past the diner and past the park and I am finally at the museum.

The sky is a doleful shade of gray, the trees an earthy shade of auburn, the same shade of oft-trampled land, colonized, stolen and hexed. The logs of the museum are too detailed in the late morning autumn sun; they remind me of the times I would do too many edibles and take walks with Nathan and Kate behind the Arseth house and into the woods. It's impossible for me to articulate *how* it made me feel, but *intimate* might be the best word. Not a cozy, sapphic intimacy like the hug from a partner; rather a night spent apologizing, inner thoughts and dysphoria rapping at your chamber door like a long forgotten ghost. I entered the main room, the windows a deep pine, cast in the hateful light of day. Mary was despondent, she was tapping her fingers against the log-walls like an alarm clock. "Wren," She said, "you're late."

"I know." I said, "I'm sorry."

"I can't tolerate this behavior. Maybe one example like this would be excusable, but seeing as how you treated those students, I think," she said, "I think it's best I let you go."

"What?" I say, my body breaking out sick with pins and needles. The walls of the museum, the taxidermy, the native art on the walls, all the goddamn angles, points of the museum that didn't feel quite right.

"You heard me," Mary said, "Thank you for the time." #

My body swarmed with sickness. I crawled back into the diner. I could commiserate with Nathan about the existential horrors of living in I-Rapids. The chrome door squealed open, 50s doo-wop blasted from the grated speakers.

"Hiya Wren," Martha said. "You feeling alright, hon?" "Could be worse," I said. "Table for one as usual." "Sure thing, hon." Martha ushered me to my seat. The fluorescent lights made me squint, everything was a puke-shade of yellow.

"Uh, is Nathan here?"

"Oh, no. I haven't seen him come in today."

"O-kay…" I said. "Just my luck." I muttered under my breath.

I sat at the table, fingering the little chrome ridges on the table. They were cold against my fingers, cooling my sickly temperament. The kitchen was short staffed, Martha walked over to me and took my order. If I didn't have a job anymore, I was sure my days of supping here would come to an end. The restaurant was bare; a chill seeped up from outside, my coat didn't do enough to shield me from the gale. I scrolled down on my phone, falling into rabbit hole after rabbit hole of bad takes.

I finished my burger and stepped outside. The sky was a vast net of purple, deep and infinitive. Mount Rainier ascended into those dreamy clouds in the October twilight. A fog came through. I propped myself against the side of the diner, fumbled in my purse for my preroll and my lighter, and did the deed. Smoke escaped the joint like a convict. The bushes rustled. *Aw fuck.* The sound oscillated, echoing like a delay pedal, a sharp *whum-whum* filling the back of my ear. My senses grew taught, my nerves were as tight as form fitting clothes. It smelled nasty, a pungent mix of rotting meat and day-old shit. Whatever, it was probably just a bear that shat in the woods, or maybe the pope. The wind was blustering, smoke rose up to my face, fogging my glasses, and coating myself in the wet, earthy aroma of cannabis.

It was getting late. I trudged back up the hill to my house, where maybe I could vent to my dad about my job, or I could work at his "Java House" as he liked to put it. I was smoking and walking at the same time, at this point more of a thing to do than an answer to my troubles. And then the wind came again, a phantom howl, a scourge and my joint went flying, careening towards the back of the diner. Money was going to be tight, I didn't want this preroll to go to waste, so I rushed after it, in the vain hope that it would still be salvageable.

Grass grew on the parking lot like the desires of a spoiled brat. The parking lot grew with tall weeds, reaching up to my ankles. The pavement was cracked and chipped. I kicked little flecks away on my quest for the joint. No luck yet. I kicked the little pebbles in the distance. *Goddamnit, what a fucking day.* A tiny thunk came from behind the diner, The rustling sounded again. I ran up to investigate, and my body went cold. My guts were a dying animal.

Despite everything it was just me, and the hairy hand lying limp against the backdoor to the diner.

When I saw Nathan's body, I whimpered, I howled, I wailed. My skin crawled with verminous pins and needles. My stomach churned, little flecks of vomit exited my mouth like drool. Lying against the side of the diner like a ragdoll was my friend, Nathan. His chest was ripped open. His guts were filled with a thick green substance. Inside his ribcage, flies made their home. It all smelled like shit, miserable, miserable shit.

"Oh no, oh god no." I was screaming, as if anybody could hear.

Nathan's eyes were scooped out, little beads of blood seeped down to his nose, mouth and beard. Rivulets of blood fell across his body. And on his head there was a big floppy, black, pointy witch hat, dancing and wobbling around in the wind. I reached for my phone, dialing 911.

"911, what's your emergency?" A woman's voice said, "H-hello..." I said.

"Yes?"

"There's... there's been a murder, I—I found a body." "Okay, where did you find this body?"

"Behind P-Pete's Diner."

"I'm sorry sir, you're breaking up."

"Behind Pete's Diner!" My voice was getting louder. "I'm sorry sir, I can't hear you."

"Behind! Pete's! Diner! The body was found in I-Rapids behind Pete's Diner!"

"I am so sorry," The operator said, "I cannot hear a word you're saying. Can you move to a place with better reception?"

"O-okay." I hung up and rushed towards the back entrance of the diner. Inside Martha was hauling a pile of plates to the dish basket. *Oh what a relief.*

"Wren are you alright?" She said, "You look like you've seen a ghost, hon."

"Nathan's body is outside, it's here, I saw it!"

"Oh no!" Dropping her plates in the basket, Martha followed me, rushing out back. Outside, wind and fog choke the parking lot like smoke-stained lungs.

"He was right here!" I said, waving my hands about, yelling, panting, my voice cracking like a pubescent boy.

"What do you mean hon?" Martha said, "I don't see anything. Probably just your imagination."

But he was right there, staring at me with those scooped-out eyes.

The bushes rustled again. In the distance like celebrants in an obscene ritual, every inch of I-Rapids encroached on me; every cracked sidewalk, every junk store, every useless fucking cryptid museum. The shadows encroached upon me.

♂

The penumbra dissipates, and we again are where we were and where we are.

For the first time, you wonder what time it is. The turning of the clock seems as distant as the windswept Plateau of Leng, where the addled spirit of a mad and waspish prophet is bound to wander forever for his prejudices in life.

"I wouldn't bother," I advise. "The more you think about it…"

You nod, remembering suddenly the cusp of puberty, remembering the hair and the dreams and the hormones pumping and bumping and burning through the body that had once upon a time seemed so uncomplicated—like a sundial suddenly evolving into a clock and bursting outward in a shower of gears when the new form could not accommodate the movement inside.

"Dysphoria is a funny word," I say, walking to the window. "It comes from the Greek 'δύσφορος', meaning 'hard to bear'." I fix you with a sharp and sudden glance. "Does it hurt?"

Does it? That one's up to you. Answer as you will.

I'll nod either way, and I'll draw open the curtains, letting in the light of a full moon that you know was waning when you left the fire. It flows over the table, turning the mugs of tea to twin ponds. "Another change then, another body with its burden to bear, baring itself in the lunar light, tearing free of itself… behold, this tale of…"

WOLFORMATION

Michelle Jacklyn Miller

✠

It was raining hard outside when I arrived at the VA hospital to see my doctor about an issue that I needed looked at. There was always something strange about me, even during my time in the army, but I had always refused to get it checked out because I didn't want it to lead to getting discharged.

I sat in my car for a moment, hoping that the rain would let up a bit, when my cell phone rang. It was an old Sprint and I flipped it open and said, "Hello?"

"Mitchell, I'm just calling to see if you made it to the doctor."

"Dad, I told you that I would call you as soon as I finished."

"Yeah, but it is raining pretty hard. I wanted to make sure you didn't get into a wreck or anything."

"No, you wanted to bug me about my condition."

"I'm just a concerned father. You know that blood in your urine can be something serious."

"Nothing that I can really say until after I see the doctor."

"I suppose that's true. So, you made it all right, I take it."

"I'm sitting in my car in front of the VA right now. Just waiting for this rain to lighten up. In fact, I think right now would be the perfect time for me to run inside."

"Alright. Talk to you later. Love you, son."

"Love you, dad." I hung up the phone. I couldn't tell my father the weirdest part about the blood in my urine. It was awkward enough telling him that I saw blood when I went to pee. He had pushed me to see the doctor, which I did with reluctance.

I had gone to the doctor last week. They ran some tests, and I was supposed to find out today what was wrong. I hadn't even told them that the bleeding in my urine was once a month, almost always exactly twenty-eight days apart. I would see blood in my urine for about one week. Then, it would go away. If I told the doctor that, they would say I was crazy. Men don't bleed rhythmically like a female period. That's what I thought they would tell me. It was best to keep the strangeness out of it and simply tell him that I saw blood in my pee.

But I always had certain female-like qualities. Anytime I ordered food over the phone, they would call me ma'am. It seemed that my voice would never get deep like typical men, and I never grew facial hair. I would go an entire week without shaving in the army, and the sergeant never noticed. I figure they thought that I shaved, or someone might have wondered what was wrong with me a lot sooner.

I suspected that I never really hit puberty. I kind of thought that I would hit would, after I got into the army when I was eighteen.Now I was twenty-one , and puberty was apparently never going to come for me. That was enough for everyone to make fun of me in the army. They said I looked like I was twelve. Or they would ask if I was wearing my big brother's uniform.

And so, I decided that I shouldn't let anyone know that I happened to be attracted to men. I didn't need to get beat up on top of everything else.

I could never have guessed that bleeding in my urine was in any way tied to my feminine qualities. When I entered the doctor's office, he had that *"Oh shit, have I got a story to tell you"* expression written all over his face. He was about to break the news to me that I had what is called Persistent Müllerian duct syndrome. I had no idea what that was, but I was about to find out.

We sat down, and he delayed the inevitable by asking how I was doing and if I was still seeing blood in my urine, which was stupid considering he had the results of my tests in his hands. He knew damn well that I still had blood in my urine, and he knew why.

"Well, you are an interesting specimen," he told me.

"I'm glad that I amuse you, doctor, but can you just tell me what is wrong with me?"

"I wouldn't call it something wrong. You have what is called Persistent Müllerian duct syndrome." Oh,*that word. I know what that is—not!*

I shook my head. "I don't have any clue what that means," I said, irritated.

"Well, it is a condition where a person who is identified as male at birth has a uterus inside. This is a condition that affects very few people to be sure."

"You are saying that I have a uterus? Like a woman?"

"Most definitely. And ovaries and fallopian tubes. Has the bleeding been on a monthly cycle by any chance?"

"Well, now that you mention it…"

"I thought so."

"But how would the blood get into my urine? Shouldn't that be… impossible?"

"It's hard to say. The uterus shouldn't even be there. Some of your tubes may have gotten crossed with something they shouldn't have. We can remove the uterus in surgery."

"What if I want to keep my uterus?"

"It could be a greater risk for cancer, but you have that right. Why would you want to keep it?"

"What if I want to get pregnant?"

"From what I see, it should be possible, but you would have to get corrective surgery. You can't very well give birth with…you know… Well, to be frank, your genitalia is kind of in the way down there."

"I need some time to think about all this." I left his office, my head swimming with emotions and thoughts. Evidently, I had hit puberty—female puberty. I had blood from a period that came once a month. The blood from my period was somehow getting into my urine.

This seemed to explain a lot about me. I had always had a desire to get pregnant. I just didn't think it was possible. We are told that a person born with a penis cannot get pregnant, but that just isn't always true. The doctor had assured me that I was not the only one who had this condition. It was rare, but it happened from time to time. The doctor had even shared one case where the person who was thought to be a man from birth not only kept the uterus, but decided to have a baby. This was the thought that intrigued me the most.

I had always been attracted to men. Perhaps, I could *transition*, as the doctor called it. I could get the penis surgically removed and get pregnant. But everything was out of sorts, he had told me. I would likely need in vitro fertilization to make it work. But I was definitely intrigued by the possibility.

I called my father and told him that the doctor didn't find anything wrong with me. It was not truly a lie, in my opinion. That is, in fact, what the doctor had said. I had just been born with female reproductive organs and a penis. My father didn't need to know about all that. I needed time to think about it.

However, little did I know, I would never get the opportunity to tell him. Another transition was just about to begin. There was going to be a full moon tonight, and I had the bright idea to go out to the bar and celebrate the possibility that I could get pregnant. Maybe, I would see an attractive man and have some fun in the process.

I arrived at the bar at around ten o'clock at night. There were a lot of guys already there. I ordered a Budweiser to get started.

That is when I noticed a man staring at me. He had dark hair, a sexy five o'clock shadow, and intense blue eyes. I was a bit uncomfortable with the way he was looking at me, as if he wanted to eat me, but I was also intrigued. He was, after all, very attractive.

I tried to ignore the staring at first. I sat there by myself and ordered two more rounds of Budweiser. Then, I looked over and noticed he was still staring at me. He wasn't even trying to hide it, so I decided to make it into a joke. I would either get rid of him or find out what he wanted.

"Are you going to stare at me all night or buy me a drink?" I asked.

He walked over to me. "I'm sorry," he whispered. "I just find you so… *delicious looking*. I could turn you into a meal."

"I don't go home with guys that I don't know very well, so you might as well buy me a couple of drinks and have some conversation."

he walked away. I was very nervous about it at this point. What if he was one of those serial killers that you hear about on the news? Suddenly, I didn't want to be there. I wanted to go home. I could find a man some other night in some other bar. This guy had really given me the creeps.

I got up and paid the bartender,then, I walked out towards my car. I looked around cautiously. If I saw that man, I was going to wait inside. When I didn't see anyone, I continued my path to my car. I opened my car door, and that is when it happened; I felt someone bite down on the back of my neck.

Blood trickled down my back and chest as pain shot through my body. I wanted to scream, but no sound would come out. When he let up, I fell to the ground.

I looked up in time to see that it was the same man that had been staring at me. He was smiling as he walked away. I was so dizzy, but I could have sworn the man had sharp teeth like a wolf. In fact, I was pretty sure that he had hair growing all over him, as if he was transforming into a… *do I dare say it?*

I crawled into my car, waited until the dizziness passed, and then somehow I drove myself home. I slept for a full day after that.

When I looked at my phone, I had more than twenty missed calls. I went to the mirror and looked at my neck. I still saw the marks where the man had bitten me.

That is when I saw something that horrified me even more. My arms had been hairless the previous day. Now, I had very dark hair all down my limbs.

I tried to go about my normal daily business,ut I began to feel a certain level of uneasiness about my body. Over the next week, I noticed that my senses had sharpened. My hearing was attuned to the hushed symphony of the night, able to detect the slightest movements and softest sounds. I became aware that every human being had a distinct scent.

I had strange dreams. I was an animal, running through a forest. I hunted prey and ate rabbits raw.

I avoided my father completely, not knowing what to say to him. I wanted to get pregnant, but I didn't want to go back to the doctor until this strange situation was resolved. I began wearing extra clothing, trying to hide all the hair that was growing. It was on my back, my chest, my arms, and my legs, everywhere!

After a week, I noticed that my hands were longer. My fingernails looked a bit more like claws. My teeth were sharper.

Then, I started sleeping all day and waking up at night. It was like I was made for the night rather than daylight. I walked outside and looked up at the sky. The moon mesmerized me. I stood there, staring at it for a long time. I had the sudden desire to howl, but I controlled myself. I looked around and saw the shadows dancing with secrets that

were whispered on the wind. That wind felt so good against my face…
and my fur.

What was happening to me?

I continued to attempt to get along in society, but there was no
doubt that some sort of strange transformation was occurring. My claws
got longer. My teeth got sharper. My fur was thicker. I tried to hide it
under the bundle of clothing that I wore, but sometimes, it felt easier to
just hide. People had begun staring at me. There was no doubt that I
was different. Even my face had started to change shapes. It started
looking more like the muzzle of a dog than a human face.

Then, one night it happened. There was a full moon out. It was
exactly one month after I had gotten bitten. I stood looking at the
moon, more mesmerized than ever. I felt my blood boiling. I started
howling and didn't care what anyone thought. A level of insanity had
struck me. I howled some more. It felt so good to howl. My hands
looked like paws, and I tore my clothes off; I wanted to be naked.

I saw that I didn't have a penis. When did that happen? I had
four paws. I leaned over on all four. I shook my head and rattled my fur.
I was a wolf, a female wolf. I ran out into the woods as fast as I could
until I came to a river. I tried to look at myself in the water.

I couldn't stand on my hind legs anymore, and the
transformation complete, I howled at the moon.

☿

The curtain closes, and we are once again enclosed in our own little world, our little space shuttle hurtling through the cosmos, locked in our little dialectic dance of spectator and spectacle. You feel the hackles on your neck relax, the hair all over your body prickling as your form once again becomes your own, your back straight, hands before your eyes and not paws. There is, somewhere in the cabin, a low, distant buzzing, like the bustling of insectile bodies crawling in the dark.

You are beginning to grow dizzy from seeing so many changes from so close up, close enough to feel inside out by the time you settle back on the cushion at the table. You do not allow yourself to settle too comfortably—you sense there are changes yet to come, wonders yet to be seen, sensations to feel and taste and explore.

"Are you afraid?" I ask. A single fly zips through the air, landing on the bloodied promotional plate.

Again the answer is your own, and you roll it over on your tongue, trying to figure out the flavor of the truth before you spill it. The buzzing is louder now.

"I only ask because it's something I miss sometimes," I say, moving towards the pantry to retrieve some crackers and summer sausage, running my hands along the stained cherrywood. "This side of the looking glass, the fourth wall, gets..." I search for my own truth, lemon-coffee bitter, slippery, and bite down ib it like a grub. "Boring isn't quite the right word. But the cycles do tend to blur together sometimes, the dharma seems to get a bit stuck and it feels like I'm left spinning the wheel, just trying to get a grip on the bits between the tellings." I consider, shaking the Magic Eight Ball. "I think the only thing that really scares me is that there's nothing left to be afraid of."

My fingers curl around the cupboard door, and when it opens, a plague of shiny black bodies flurries out of the cupboard, turning the room sootdark, and they obscure our shapes, my mouth opening, my voice one with the droning scream of the legion of wings:

"Sometimes you wake up," the flies sing, "sometimes the fall kills you... and sometimes, when you fall, you..."

FLY

Madeleine Varley

✠

My skin hurts. I'm leaning over my parents sink, decidedly ignoring my reflection in the mirror. My hands shake, I'm barely able to hook my fingers under the rough bandages on my back.

"You're selfish, you know that? All we ever wanted was the best for you!" My dad shouts, his voice accompanied by the thud of his fist against the other side of the wooden door. I wince at his words and take a few shaking breaths. My shoulders rise and fall too much, curved in on myself as I try to get my body back under my control. The sink is half full from the morning's preparations, and slowly dripping more water into the bowl. There's a cup on the edge of the sink, one I made when I was little. My eyes trace the familiar curves, following them swirling up the side.

I made it when I was six. I came home that night with it clutched in my little hands and gave it to my mother for her birthday. That was when I got the bindings for the first time. I had woken up in the middle of the night, all I could register was the way my back felt strange. I ran my fingers along my spine as far as I could reach and bounced my way to my parents room. They ran their hands over my back, gasping and whispering to each other, and finally calling the doctor. The doctor muttered to himself and then to my parents and I sat there, staring at the mug on my mothers bedside table and swinging my legs. Only later did my father fill me in shakily. There was something growing out of my back. They would bind it, keep it from growing, but I couldn't tell anyone. It would ruin our family, my father said. I agreed, what else could I say? But it hurt. I thrashed and turned in my sleep, complaining to my parents during the day, but they refused to take it off.

Years went by. Bandages were replaced by others, cloth was

layered over bandages and shirts were tailored to hide my back. My mother grew distant. The mug was moved to the bathroom. My father worked. I cried to them, they said it was for the best.

The crack of the door startles me back to the present. My eyes snap towards the sound and it comes again. My dad's voice disappeared, it looks like he's ramming through the door. My breath quickens, and I glance in the mirror to finish the job I started out to do. The bandage on my back had grown tight, and if I turned to the side I could just see where it sprouted out of my back. It hurts, it always hurts. It feels like a fire bubbling under my skin, constantly. With a final breath I hook my fingers under the adhesive and pull it off in one quick move.

I'm screaming. Or at least, I think I am. I want to. My skin is breaking, I can feel it, ripping jagged slits from my back. I claw at myself, wherever I can reach, my ragged nails catching on my pale skin, drawing thin red lines over my arms, legs, chest, throat. My voice feels like nails against my throat, a shrill cry bouncing off of the walls in the suddenly too-small bathroom. My nails catch wherever they can reach, I can feel my body writhing against the wood floor, but it feels distant compared to the agony my own body has turned against me.

"What the fuck did you do?" My fathers voice manages to cut through the pain. I look at him, his form a blur through the tears that cloud my vision. My mother is there too, just behind him, and she lets out a quiet sob, clutching my fathers arm with one hand and a cooking knife in the other, she looks as if she was interrupted in the middle of cooking dinner. I scramble away from them, barely able to control my body as I hunch in on myself. I'm a cornered animal, my parents disgusted horror showing on their faces as my vision clears.

"What have you done to my baby?" My mother gasped in a near-whisper. My fathers away, and she steps up in front of him.

"No, no, mama-" I beg. I need help, can't they see that? It hurts so much, I can barely think. I reach for her, a last, desperate plea, but she brandishes the knife at me. "I am not your mother. My daughter would never do this," She hisses. Do I look that wrong? Did I make that big of a mistake? It hurt under the bandages, but this is so much worse. My body falls forwards with a sob as the thing under my skin pushes further out, forcing me away from the wall I tried to push into. My parents say something to each other, quickly, and I see them moving away.

"No, please!" I scream, lunging forwards with a speed I didn't know I had. My mother cries out and my father pulls her back, away from me. He grabs the knife from her and puts himself between me and my mother. I slam my hand over my mouth, stifling the next scream and curling in on myself. My parents are gone the next time I look up.

I don't know how long I stayed there, curled in on my side, my body shaking with pain and exhaustion. I can't move. Tears stain my cheeks. I'm staring at the wooden floor, my forehead pressed against it. Slowly, slowly I realize that the pain has subsided. I look up but my head bursts in a sharp pain at the new way my eyes move. The edges of my vision blur as I glance around the room. The forms were too sharp and the colors too bright, and I was forced to bury my head back into my arms to keep my mind from breaking. I breathe in, holding the air tight in my chest, and slowly let it out through my teeth. I stand.

It's awkward, standing when there's something unnatural on my back. I lean forwards, trying to counteract the new weight on my back, and am forced to grab the bowl of the sink to stop myself from falling. Slowly my eyes drift upwards, the edges still blurring, and they land on my face. I look pale, gaunt and unnatural. Lines of blood snake down my sides and from deep scrapes I must have inflicted on myself. A shiver moves down my back and into the new objects sprouting from it.

They're large. There's two of them, though they're bumping into each other as if forced into a space too small for them. Slowly, tentatively, I realize I can spread them. The left one follows my thought, reaching out behind me, spreading. With a quiet gasp;

"Wings," I whisper to myself. They're not feathered or bat-like, they're fleshy and I can see my bones pushing out under them. They hurt to move, like stretching out legs after a run or arms after a long day's work. I wonder, quietly to myself, why this was ever such a bad thing? They are beautiful, my wings. If my parents can't see that then that's their fault, and how it hurt them! These wings, my wings, they are the most beautiful thing I've ever seen. I spread them and laugh, I would go through that pain again and again for these few precious moments with my wings.

The door downstairs creaks open and I jump. There's heavy footsteps and shouting, though I can't make out the words. Their voices seem foreign to me, too sharp and rough, but it sounds like too many people. My breath catches in my throat and I force my gaze away from my reflection. My mind reels again, with the weight of the sharpened world around me, and I turn to the window. This is technically the second floor, but it isn't that high up I reason to myself. I could survive the drop and- and if my wings work then- The voices are closer, too close. I'm running out of time. My breath grows quick and my lungs burn. I take a deeper breath, bounce on the balls of my feet, and, as the first figure rounds the corner, throw myself through the window.

I'm falling, but everything feels too slow. The greenery around me seems to assault my eyes, too bright compared to the dull world I'm used to seeing. It feels as if I'm floating down through water. My body reacts on its own, my wings unfurl.

It's awful. And it's amazing, and it's like nothing I've ever felt before. My body jolts up as I catch the wind, but I'm barely able to control myself as it only slows my descent. I hit the ground and roll, my arms reaching up to cover my head as I slow to a stop. I hear the voices above me still, but more than that voices near me and next to me and

I jump to standing, my eyes wide as they catch everything around me. Half the town must be here, god do they think I'm that dangerous? Why would my parents do this? I open my mouth but nothing comes out, just a low sound that I didn't think I was able to make. The people around me adjust, some making sounds of disgust or horror, or just awe and disbelief. My shoulders hunch and the noise grows louder, more like a growl than any human noise I realize.

Someone brandishes a knife at me and I step back. The forest presses against my house, my parents house. Maybe I could lose them in the woods?

A gunshot echoes somewhere near me and I reel back, hitting a tree and falling to the ground over its roots. My breath is quick and shallow in my chest. My hands scrabble for purchase on the loose dirt. I can't be here. I manage to get my mind back in control, confirming with myself, no I'm not shot, yes it must have been just the surprise or the sound that startled me, and I'm up again. I'm not wearing shoes, I realize, but it doesn't matter. I push off trees to avoid hitting them, dashing through the woods like the deer I've hunted. I can still hear the voices behind me, but I'm faster, I know. My new vision picks up every change, every twist in the dirt and I bound over roots and rocks that would have caused me to slip before now. I laugh, loud and sharp. Maybe it's bloodloss, I don't care. This is who I was meant to be, yes this is me. This figure with wings and vision that no human is supposed to have, this is what my parents kept from me. They were ruining me.

I notice the change before it happens, but still only avoid running off the cliff by impulse, grabbing a branch and hurling my weight down. My knee hits the ground and I use the momentum to whirl back to face the people running after me. I knew there was a cliff, but it should have taken longer to get here. I can just barely see the figures in the distance approaching, but they're approaching fast. I back slowly towards the cliff. I have wings, this should be an easy choice, I think to myself. I'm angry, angry at myself for not having what it takes to trust my new body. I could fly.

Or I could fall.

The thought feels sick, leftover from someone who is not me. That is the girl's thinking, the girl who bound the best part of herself just because her parents asked her too, not my thinking. I want to yell at her, tell her to trust me, but there is only so much I can do in my own mind. I let out a bark of anger as the people catch up to me. I'm out of time. Now or never.

I turn and, in the same movement, jump. It's all I can do. I let out an inhuman scream as I begin to plummet towards the ground. But I'm who I am supposed to be. I trust myself, I think, I whisper in a language I'm supposed to speak, I trust myself.

My wings unfurl.

△

The buzzing subsides, the black bodies wriggling through the cracks in the windows and the doors until there is once again only silence between us. The magpie, rattled, flutters over to my bed, and begins pecking at my pillow.

"Hey!" I say, grabbing a pear from the bowl on the table and chucking it at the bird.

You touch your shoulder with ginger caution, as if expecting to feel the rough cotton of bandages, but instead only touch the fabric of your screen-printed Brook Pridemore shirt. The sensation of falling, falling, falling cradles and coddles you, like your wires have been cut and you're hurtling towards the ground even as you can feel the floor of the winnebago under your feet.

"The flies were only a scourge for the Egyptians, you know," I say, fetching the crackers from the shelf, safe in their metal tin. The sausage had been laid to waste, so I brought out a jar of blood orange and fig jam instead. "They were a miracle for the frogs." Setting them on the table, I pull a butter knife from the dishrack, sticking it into the preserves so the handle stuck up like the waiting sword of a destined boy-king. "More tea with your jam?"

You nod as you take the knife in hand, spreading it over the salt-speckled surface of the cracker, peering up at you like an unblinking button eye. When you have adorned your unleavened bread, I decorate my own to match, and we hold the crackers up in a toast before imbibing together.

We taste the fruit and the flowers as one, swapping spit without touching tongues or even lips, lost in communion, and beneath the sweet is the taste of burning chrome. As the popping sugar envelopes us both in a haze of glistening static, again my mouth begins its tireless, tithing duty: "Taste, if you will, a teleological technology of terror, a treacherous trade and a trodden trail through a digital nightmare, a computational error that leaves one exchanging the finest..."

FIGS FOR THISTLES

E. B. Novetti

�⚭

I. Behind us, beyond us, the electric desert was a perennial night, reddened in the far west by a sun that never set, because to travel east into the desert was to travel sticky through time, back to the beginning at the end of the road. The farther you got on the road, the more time stretched and slowed, pulling like taffy, until at the point of origin you crossed the unknown boundary into somewhere so good that you forgot about the fact that you were a discard and a fuck-up and that you'd signed up for virtual reality because you couldn't think of anywhere better to go. Or so Dex and I supposed. Any day now we could collide with some invisible limit.

But for now, we were making progress. The road was a broad grid, which undulated with rainbow lights that flashed in time with the theme music. The desert was sand, desolate aside from the tracks of skittering electric lizards. If you caught a lizard underfoot, it electrocuted you until you fell down dead. Then you rematerialized in the middle of the road, a long distance behind where you'd been, although distance was a term that said little in a landscape without time or scope.

Mostly I measured distance according to how annoyed Dex was as they waited for me to catch up to them. By this metric, my latest encounter with a lizard had sent me very, very far away. I checked the map for Dex's position, which blinked like a tiny red star. I was always getting electrocuted because I was always making excursions into the desert, where the lizards were.

When I reached Dex, they started the old argument. I'd never heard Dex's voice. When they spoke, their words appeared in white type at the bottom of my visual field: "There's nothing out there. If you don't stop trekking into the desert, we'll never get to the end."

"We don't know what's at the end," I said. "We don't even know that there is an end." I was glad Dex couldn't hear me. They encountered my voice the same way I encountered theirs: as a series of tiny ephemeral billboards.

"O ye of little faith," responded Dex.

Once in a while something good happened, like when we found two cars abandoned on the side of the road. We started driving, and the desert theme music sped up and grew a bassline as the cars skated over the rainbow grid. As we weaved and swerved, the road rippled with squares of light, and the music grew louder and louder until I hit euphoria. It didn't last long; the cars' speed dwindled until finally they just stopped. We stayed awhile to see if the cars would draw a charge from the ground somehow, but they never did.

Sometimes a desert fox ran across the road. Out of habit, I'd shoot it with my arrow and attempt to put it in my pack to eat later, but my pack was always full, because I had never gotten hungry in the desert. Dex found dead foxes distasteful.

Another time, Dex stopped talking to me.

"Dex," I said. "You have to talk to me sometime. Unless you want to go back to the start of all this so I can find somebody else to talk to."

"I don't know if we could even make it back at this point," they wrote.

"We talked about this already," I said. "If we used the lizards to kill ourselves, we can cover a lot of distance. We'd be back to the beginning in no time."

"I don't think you can get out that way," they responded. "I don't think this will ever end."

And it didn't end, although when lightning storms came, it felt like it might. There was never rain, but we put up a tent made of rubber, to absorb the current in case we got struck by lightning. During the storms we used to describe sex to each other and masturbate. That

was how I found out that Dex's other body, their physical body, was a
man's. In virtual reality, their avatar was tall and sexless, with a curved
sword at each hip and a black veil that they never took off, except
during the storms. The veil covered everything but their black eyes.

Lately we'd stopped talking about sex. Now when a storm
came we told stories about our lives before and what we'd find at the
end of the road. Once I told them about how I'd entered gameplay. The
game facilitators offered me one year. I signed up for ten.

But Dex never told me who they'd been or where their body
was housed in the real world. The only thing they said was that they
grew up on a dairy farm in Iowa. I didn't pry. I'd learned before I met
Dex that it was bad manners to ask. The whole point of virtual reality
was to get away from reality, and everyone I'd met in VR was an elective
amnesiac. We wanted to forget that we were the people for whom
various institutions exist: asylums, prisons, shelters, "homes."

I wasn't sure which category fit Dex. They might have been
some kind of schizo, whose visits to the mental hospital had failed to
fix them. They definitely weren't coming from rehab— they didn't have
the social skills to get into drugs. But the most likely scenario was that
they were one of those kids whose parents lock them in closets, or
something like that. I'd once asked, jokingly, if they'd always dreamed of
being a ninja warrior when they grew up. "No," Dex replied, "I dreamt
of being an animal."

When the lightning storms ended we emerged from the tent
and watched the storm recede across the desert. This time it was blue
lightning, which traveled north to south. The orange lightning went the
other way, from south to north, and the multi-colored lightning, which
was my favorite, came from the east, where we were headed, and passed
over us and behind, where we'd come from.

And then, one day, Dex snapped their fingers in front of my
face as I stood dumbfounded in front of a door that hung midair two
feet past the end of the road.

Dex's words appeared: "I'll let you do the honors." I didn't ask Dex what wonderful thing we'd find on the other side of the door. Whatever it was, we had earned it.

❦

II. Through the doorway was a forest, neon with life. The portal dissolved as soon as we'd crossed it. For a minute I couldn't do anything but just stand there. The desert theme music had stopped. Without theme music, it was like I was back in real life, except that I wasn't.

"Dex," I whispered, "Can you smell it?"

"Yes," they responded.

"Does your console have that kind of tech? Smell? Mine doesn't," I said.

It smelled like forests do, clean and alive. All around us slender gray trunks rose skyward. Sunlight filtered through spring leaves. On either side of the dirt trail where we'd materialized, ferns susurrated in the breeze. I was delirious, pulsing with the happiness of it, manic with sunlight. I breathed in the fragrant air and sat on the ground. Dex decided it was an opportunity to conduct a thorough inspection of the ferns.

"All the ferns are modeled on the same species," reported Dex.

"I'm going to look around," I said.

I'd forgotten the luminescence of forests, how sun could limn the trees like lustrous fog. Every few minutes I checked my map for Dex's location. They were exactly where I'd left them. At last I arrived at a clearing. In the middle of the clearing was a table set with porcelain dishes, and in the center of the table sat a woman in a diaphanous pink gown. She propped her chin on one fist and gazed into the treetops with a dreamy look on her face. "Hello?" I said. I stepped toward her. Forest birdsong changed to lilting harp music as my visual field locked to exposition mode. As my vision narrowed to a close-up of the woman's face, she giggled to herself, then startled theatrically.

"Oh! I didn't see you there. Welcome to my forest," she said. A baritone voice rang in my ears as simultaneously the words appeared in pink type at the bottom of my visual field. "I am the Salvo Salvation, and I'd like to tell you my story," she continued, "but before I begin—"

I backed away, which triggered a suspension of exposition mode. It was usual to encounter a story-teller in every new village or realm. Story-tellers were part of the game. Their job was to give you quests, introduce you to other players, or otherwise keep your life interesting. But it had been a long time since I'd encountered anyone besides Dex. "There's someone up there," I said once I'd reached them.

They studied me, black eyes just visible behind his veil. When they looked at me that way, I felt like we were married.

"She can probably tell us where we are," they said.

Ⓘ

When Dex and I reached the clearing, we stepped together towards the table, which triggered exposition mode. Exactly as she had the first time, the woman in the pink gown giggled to herself, then startled.

"Oh! I didn't see you there. Welcome to my forest," she said in the same deep voice. Pink type materialized and dematerialized. "I am the Salvo Salvation, and I'd like to tell you my story, but before I begin, will you accept my invitation to dinner?"

"Do you think we should?" I whispered to Dex. "We haven't looked around much. What if we're supposed to talk to someone else first?"

"No," said Dex. "This is it. This is the end of the road." They pulled a chair from the table and sat.

The Salvo Salvation smiled and turned to me.

"Sit," said the Salvo Salvation, so I did. Her canned laughter sounded again. My avatar evaporated as my visual field descended through white clouds into a mountain landscape. All around me I heard a heartbeat.

"Dex?" I said.

The scene before me now was unscripted: two scrawny, dirty teenagers—a girl and a boy, the two hardly distinguishable—scrabbled around a hair-pin turn as they followed a steep mountain trail.

I come from an old place, began the Salvo Salvation. Pink typeface appeared in my peripheral vision against the backdrop of sepia dirt and flaxen mountain grasses. Until the story ended, we were hers.

III. I come from an old place, said the Salvo Salvation, a fertile valley in the shadow of arid mountains, where I lived with my twin brother, Jupiter, among fields of grain that rippled in the wind that came down from the mountain.

The year my mother died, Jupiter became head of the family. My brother was stupid, my brother was lazy and inept, but it was my twin, Jupiter—lazy, foolish, feeble-minded Jupiter— who my village accorded authority over the family—if one unsatisfactory twin sister could be called a family. Jupiter became my keeper.

I walked along the river that bordered the village and fantasized that I was someone else—somewhere else. What relief it would be to wade across the river that bordered the village—to keep walking until I reached a place where no one knew me.

Then one, day the locusts came.

The first locust was as large as my palm, with glittering eyes and a body almost exactly the same color as the stalk of grain to which it clung. Jupiter lay on his back on the grassy bank of the river, and when he couldn't be convinced to get up, I took his scythe from the house and went to our field myself, to save what grain I could.

By the midday, it was upon us. Locusts crawled in my hair and clung to my dress until I ran back to the house. We hung blankets in the windows and doors, but nothing could keep the locusts out. They crawled on the beds; I could not walk without stepping on one. Hordes of them flew into the water jug, their wings beating noisily against the walls of the jug until they finally drowned.

Before the week was out they'd devoured everything. Around the village, a few fields were black with ash where people had burned them hoping to drive the insects away. The rest of the fields were stripped clean. A handful of glitter-eyed stragglers clung to ravished stalks, their jaws working continuously.

The village council called meetings with the silo-keeper, while everyone else collected as many locusts—dead or alive—as we could. We roasted them in hot embers, or pulled off the hind-legs and ate them whole, or ground them into a fine powder to store for the coming weeks. Although the supply of locusts seemed endless, we all knew that it was not. When we ran out, there'd be nothing left but the chickens and the grain stored in the communal silo.

It was no surprise to me when the silo-keeper arrived at the conclusion that a messenger from the village should be sent to the monastery on the mountain to seek guidance, nor was it a surprise when the village council decided that each family in the village would be allowed a say before the council decided whom to send.

☿

As Jupiter and I neared the square in the dimming twilight, I heard voices in the midst of a full-fledged discussion. I shoved Jupiter a little and motioned for him to hurry up; he raised a pacifying hand in response. I fought the urge to kick him. At last we emerged into the crowded square. I caught a fragment of the widow Leah's speech ("...it makes the most sense...") before she looked around and saw us. The widow made a show of deference to Jupiter. "Where's your son?" I asked Leah.

"He's gone to scout for game."

"He'd be very lucky to find anything this time of year," I said.

"He's a gifted hunter," she answered.

I opened my mouth to respond, but at that moment the village council emerged from the meeting house on the far side of the square. The small crowd fell silent. I noticed people glancing at Leah.

"I speak for my family," said Leah.

"The council recognizes the widow Leah," answered the head councilman.

"The journey to the monastery is an honor," said Leah. "It's also dangerous. It would be best to safeguard as many of our villagers as possible."

Other villagers nodded.

"Perhaps—" I began.

"Do you speak for your family?" asked one of the councilmen.

"Yes, I speak for my family," I said. "It's true that the journey is dangerous. But the council determined that it's the best course of action. No one but the monks can help us determine a safe path. If our survival depends on the success of the journey, wouldn't the best way to safeguard as many villagers as possible be to send a messenger who has the greatest chance of success?"

"Wise words for someone so young," said the head councilman. Jupiter stole a jealous glance at me.

"If success is crucial, wouldn't it be better to send a group?" said Jupiter.

"It would certainly be wise to send more than one person," said Leah.

"Caravans are slow," said another councilman. "We can't spare that many people. We need as many people as possible to gather and hunt what they can."

"We'll need hunters," agreed Leah. "In fact—"

"So we're agreed," I interrupted, "that it's best to send just one person, and this person should be someone with enough experience to—"

"What if we sent a smaller party?" said someone.

"Or even just a couple of people." Leah glanced at me.

"Two people wouldn't have the safety of a caravan."

"He's just said we can't spare a caravan," said Jupiter.

"It would have to be two people who could be spared, two people who—" said Leah. "What about the twins?"

"They're very young."

"Everyone know Jupiter is worthy of the undertaking," said Leah. "Besides—"

"I'm not even a woman yet," I argued.

"No one asked you," hissed Jupiter.

"—the twins have only one soul between them," finished Leah. "If only one were to die, the village would be robbed of nothing." According to traditional beliefs, Jupiter and I shared just one soul between us because we'd emerged from the same womb on the same day. "That old superstition?" said the head councilman.

Leah glanced around for support. "Isn't that what the monks taught our ancestors? Why would we send anyone at all up the mountain if we don't believe the monks' teachings?"

"It would be an honor," said Jupiter, the fool. "Does the council accept our service?" The head councilman said, "If we all agree."

There were mutters of assent around the square.

"But—" I began.

Jupiter glared at me. If there were some way to escape, it had already slipped through my fingers.

I'd planned to stay silent until we reached the safety of our house, but we were arguing as soon as we were out of the other villagers' earshot.

"No one in their right mind would climb those mountains," I berated Jupiter. "Travelers follow the river, they stay near fertile land, they—"

"Well, it might be difficult, but that's not the point," he said. "It's an honor."

"An *honor*?" I spat. "It's a death sentence, you moron. Who do you know who's made that journey and come back? Who's going to protect our share of grain from the silo while we're gone?"

"If there's a monastery up there, it must be possible to make the journey," he reasoned. "And how do you know there is a monastery? How do you know the stories about the monks who taught us all the old rituals aren't a bunch of lies invented to scare children?"

"What?" he said, blinking. I shut my eyes in frustration. It was one thing to trust stories and the people who told them, but my brother was no true believer. Rather, he was so literal minded that no thought of a world beyond his immediate reality had ever occurred to him.

A day later, Jupiter and I set out with little fanfare. The mountain was too steep to climb directly. Instead, we trudged up the trail that hair-pinned back and forth up the mountainside. Every so often the trail diverged, and then we'd stand at the crossroads and bicker about which way to go until Jupiter threw his pack onto the ground and lay in the dust with his hands over his eyes. By the end of the first day I already hated him.

We slept fitfully beside a fire built from grasses and what little wood we'd been able to gather near the campsite. The first burned fast and bright; every time we began to drift off, it died down again and a miserable cold stole inside our blankets.

The next day, as we stopped at yet another rocky outcropping to catch our breath, I spotted a goat. She chewed placidly on a tuft of brown grass just below the outcropping. I pulled out an arrow and threaded my bow.

"It's bad luck," said Jupiter.

"You'll scare her away," I whispered. "What does it matter if goats are sacred? I'm hungry."

I held the goat in sight. Her rib bones, like my own, were clearly visible beneath her skin. Dust clung to her legs and her wooly coat where it hung down from her belly. She leapt across the rocks and out of sight.

℘

It was supposed to take three days to reach the monastery. It had been five days and we'd seen no sign. We were almost out of food. My shoes had dug into my feet until they had blistered and oozed.

"We have to be close by now," I panted. Jupiter didn't look up. He was too tired to care. The muscles in my legs ached, a relentless wrenching pain.

We turned a corner and the trail suddenly lost its steepness. We reached a plateau. I collapsed onto the flat ground, close to tears, too tired to take off my pack. I rolled onto my side to look at a stone wall on the far side of the plateau.

It had to be the monastery. Somewhere in that wall there was a hidden entrance. I closed my eyes and rested my head against the ground. My mind wandered to the food the monks would have for us, the warm beds.

The ground thrummed with a sound like a cantering horse. I

looked up. A figure, clothed in a long, hooded monk's cassock, sent up clouds of dust as he approached us. "Jupiter," I said. Jupiter opened his eyes and pushed himself into a sitting position. Then the man was upon us.

"Hello," said the monk in the quavery voice of an old man. But he was not a man at all. Under the shadow of the hood, his face was a goat's, with staring eyes the color of spring grasses. His pupils were rectangular slashes, which gave him—like all goats—an expression both vacant and clever. His bearded neck disappeared into the cowl of his gray tunic, but underneath the robe he had shoulders like a man's. Emerging from the shadows at the end of his billowing sleeves were two hands—human hands, though exceptionally hairy.

My breath caught in my chest. There was the grinding noise of pebbles against hard earth as Jupiter scrabbled backward. With inhuman agility, the goat-man crossed the rocky terrain between us and grabbed my pack, dragging me roughly so that my my bare shins scraped painfully across the rocky ground.

"Let me go!" I screamed as Jupiter fumbled to string his bow.

"Ah, you can speak," said the creature, who had already released me. "That will make things easier. What brings you here?"

"Our village sent us," I said. "We're supposed to ask for the abbot."

"I'll bring him," said the goat-man. "Don't wander."

He turned and walked back the way he'd come.

"What was that thing?" muttered Jupiter when the goat-man had disappeared from view.

"A monk, I guess," I answered.

Jupiter sat on the ground again. "Do you think all the monks are that way?" he said. I didn't respond, because there was no conceivable answer. I took off my pack, careful not to touch the raw skin on my shoulders as I pulled down the straps.

People in the village sometimes told stories during the early dark of winter nights. There were outlandish tales about far-off cities, and fables about the first inhabitants of the village. There were also stories about creatures—the blind women who lived in the riverbed, or talking hawks large enough to carry off disobedient children. In the dream of their telling I believed all these stories, but in the daytime world, I put them away again.

I rolled onto my back and looked up, away from the blinding mountain peaks and toward the open sky. My chest rose and fell. There were goat-men. Some stories were real, then, even when daylight came.

I closed my eyes and drifted until I heard footsteps. The goat-man had returned. There were two more goat-men with him, one in white robes and the other in orange. I sat up as the orange-robed monk approached us. Beneath his hood, this creature had a large, black head and a goatish neck, thicker than a man's, that sloped into broad shoulders. His vacant yellow eyes fixed first on Jupiter's face and then on mine.

"My name is Brother Theos," he said. "I'm the abbot."

He gestured toward our packs and the white-robed monk leapt towards us, more nimbly than a man could have, and seized my pack and then Jupiter's.

"The postulant will carry your things," continued Brother Theos. "I understand you've asked to speak with me. Presumably you seek guidance. We'll get to that in due time. Can you walk?"

I rose painfully from the ground. It was, at least, a little easier without the extra weight of my pack. As we followed Brother Theos towards the high wall in the distance, the other two monks trailed behind us. Theos continued to talk.

"Our monastery observes silence," he said. "Once we take our final vows, we don't speak except in prayer or, as now, when it's necessitated by circumstance. However, as guests, you're not required to follow our laws."

As we approached the wall, I distinguished an arched doorway.

"Speak freely between yourselves, but do not expect our brothers to converse," continued Theos.

We passed under the shadow cast by the doorway in the wall. Then we were on a cobblestone street that led into a town constructed atop the terraced mountainside. My blistered feet struck the cobblestones painfully as the monks proceeded down the street with a clatter of hooves against stone.

Here and there, more monks—mostly in dun-colored robes like the one who'd discovered us, but a few in white—cantered along the street or bent over austere gardens. A postulant, his robes painfully white in the sunlight, led a four-legged goat down the street by a rope around her neck.

"There are goats here," I said.

"We keep them for their wool, among other purposes," said Theos.

"We saw a goat like that while we were coming up the mountain," I said. "People in the village think they're sacred."

"You speak at length," said Theos.

Finally we stopped in front of a low building with an arched doorway. There was no door. The postulant entered at once and set down our things.

"You'll sleep here. Before we depart, give your rations to Brother Gerard," said Theos. He indicated the old, gray-robed monk who had found us. "He'll bring them to the kitchens, so that we can prepare them for your evening meal."

"The village didn't have much food to spare," said Jupiter. "We ran out yesterday."

"Couldn't you spare us some food?" I said to Theos.

"We keep some salt and other medicinals, but nothing else your kind would call food," he said. "We have no use for it. We sustain ourselves from the mountain grasses." He fell quiet. I was overcome with despair, huge and irresistible as nightfall. "You are hungry and therefore distressed," he observed. He chewed his cud, then continued, "One of your kind visited here several seasons ago. He died shortly afterward. We stored his things. Perhaps he carried something that you would find edible." Here he paused, as if to allow us a moment to appreciate his providence, then continued, "For now you should rest. Someone will come for you later."

Jupiter and I went inside. Two beds stood on opposite walls. Across from the doorway, a clay basin sat on a large stone shelf protruding from the wall. I ripped my shoes painfully from the congealed blood on my feet, washed myself, and fell asleep.

I opened my eyes to see Jupiter standing over me.

"Someone's come," he muttered. He nodded toward the open doorway. A white-robed postulant stood just outside. "He said he's here to bring us to Brother Theos." He stole a nervous glance at the monk's silhouette. "He stopped talking after that."

The postulant had a goat's face, no more or less monstrous than Brother Theos's, but his stare was unsettling. He beckoned for us to follow him.

Outside, my bare feet curled painfully around cold, bulbous cobblestones. The night sky was sharper here, the stars more luminous. It was as if I'd only ever seen stars through a film of scum, and now I saw them clearly for the first time.

At last the postulant rapped on the side door of a narrow stone building.

"Enter," came the muffled reply from within. The postulant pushed open the door and gestured for us to go inside.

A half-dozen candles burned in small candle-holders affixed to the walls. Despite the candlelight, the room was darker than the moonlit street. Brother Theos stood behind a tall table. The faces of the goat-men all looked the same to me—I couldn't tell two goat-men apart any better than I could distinguish two blades of grass—but Theos was recognizable by his orange abbot's robes.

"I've brought you here to provide instructions before our meal," he said.

"You've found food for us, then?" I said.

"The brotherhood takes their meals together," he said. "We eat in the dining hall. We do not converse. I ask that you also refrain from speaking. You'll sit at the postulants' table. You may find our dining room ill-suited to your needs. We've attempted accommodations, but we don't often host your kind."

He fixed his yellow stare on me and continued, "I ask also that you maintain a modest attitude throughout your time here, and especially during meals. Have respect for our postulants, who are young and vulnerable to temptation. To them you are exotic creatures, and they may harbor certain unnatural fascinations."

I averted my eyes and nodded.

"Now you'll accompany me to the dining hall," he said. He took one lit candle from the wall and blew out the rest before he led us into a dark hallway.

Inside the dining hall, monks had already assembled at tables as high as my shoulders. Some of them pressed their hands together in silent prayer; others hid their hands in voluminous sleeves. Still others stood with their arms at their sides.

Theos' hooves rang loudly against the flagstone as we followed him across the room. Most of the monks ignored Jupiter and me, but every now and then one of them stared curiously. After what seemed like a long time, we arrived at a table of fidgeting, white-robed postulants. There were two empty places directly across from each other. Instead of chairs, two crates had been overturned on the floor, apparently for us to stand on.

Theos gestured towards our places. I climbed onto my crate, and although the table was still too high to be comfortable, I was at least within arm's reach of my plate, where three cornmeal cakes and greens were already arranged. Next to me, the monks' plates were piled with brown grasses. I wanted very badly to eat, but the monks were waiting, so I did too.

Eventually Theos reached his table and his clacking footsteps ceased. His voice echoed through the room: "Let us pray."

The monks joined hands at once. I raised my hand and felt the goat-man beside me grasp it. His grip was warm and dry, almost human.

The brothers recited a prayer in an unfamiliar language. When the prayer ended, the monks immediately shoved grass into their mouths with their large, hairy hands. I'd expected them to eat with the same disciplined grace that attended their other actions, but they ate just like goats: long tufts of grass protruded from their lips as they chewed noisily. It seemed like their mouths never stopped moving.

Jupiter and I ate with our hands, too, and when dinner ended, a postulant led us back to our room.

𝑣

The next morning I went into the street and walked aimlessly.

My mind looped through the same few thoughts. We'd reached the monastery, but they had little food for us. We consumed more of this limited quantity at every meal. There was no other food except the goats, but slaughtering them was probably even more taboo here than it was in our village.

I had no further information. I tried to recall anything my mother had told me about the mountain—any plants or animals that might be good to eat—but I couldn't remember her ever telling me anything about the mountains except the fact that monks lived there and cities lay beyond them. I wandered until my feet hurt too much to continue, and then I hobbled back to the room, regretting with each step that I hadn't followed Jupiter's example and gone back to the room directly after breakfast.

Ɛ

A few hours after I got back to our room, a postulant messenger arrived in the doorway. Jupiter and I followed him to the building where Theos had given us instructions the night before.

In the daylight I saw that room where we'd received instructions from Theos was an office. The floor was covered with woolen rugs in various sober shades; the walls were lined with bookshelves. Brother Theos stood behind the desk, eyes fixed on the pages of an enormous leather-bound book.

""Why did your village send you here?" he said. He closed the book.

"Locusts," answered Jupiter.

"A swarm ate the crop, and now we're facing famine. The council wants guidance," I added. "They said you had divination rites that might help us choose the wisest course of action."

"It's part of the Brotherhood's vows to offer guidance to those who seek it," said Theos. "I'll make good on our vows. However, we're faced with certain material difficulties."

"Food," I said.

"Yes," he said. "As I told you before, we had another visitor recently. He came better prepared than you did, but still, he carried a limited amount of food. I don't think he planned to stay here long. The two of you will consume his rations within ten days."

"What about your goats?" I said. "Are they good to eat?"

Theos stared. "I'm sure you meant no harm," he said, "but slaughtering our nannies is forbidden. I urge you not to mention it again. Our laws notwithstanding, the herd that we keep may yet provide an answer to your difficulties."

He drummed his fingers on the book's leather cover. I wondered which animal, if not the goats, had been skinned to make the leather.

"How do you mean?" I said.

"Their milk," he said, as if it were obvious. "But we don't have any nursing mothers at the moment. The birthing season is weeks away. However, the monk who husbands the herd has informed me that there is a nanny whose pregnancy appears to have gone awry. We believe that she'll enter labor soon. If she doesn't, we'll induce it. Once she gives birth, there's a chance that she could be encouraged to give milk."

"And you'd give the milk to us," I said.

"The brothers have discussed the matter. We agree that this confluence of unusual circumstances suggests that divine will intends for the milk to sustain you," he said.

"But there's a chance it won't work?" I said.

"That's why I've summoned you here," he said. "We'll wait five days for the nanny to enter labor. At the end of five days, we will induce labor if it hasn't already begun. Births, once started, are usually quick, but let's say six days until we can ascertain her ability to give milk." "If it doesn't work, we'd have only four days' worth of food left," I said.

"But we can't go back to the village," said Jupiter. "Not without—"

"I'm not suggesting you return," said Brother Theos. "If you were to leave the monastery, it would be wiser to seek sustenance somewhere besides your village. We might be able to provide some guidance, but any journey, you understand, would require many days of travel."

Jupiter and I glanced at each other.

"Now you understand my intent. I want to make your choice clear. You're free to take the remaining rations and depart right now, in hopes that you'll have a better chance of survival. You're also at liberty to stay here until the birth."

"Can't you tell us what to do?" I said. "Can't you divine the future?"

"Divination rites require lengthy preparation," he said. "The ceremonies that may help guide the future of your village, for example, will require many weeks."

"Why? Why can't you do it now?" I said. Brother Theos caressed the leather book and looked through windows at the front of the room.

"The rite depends on the participation of one of our goats. She is very special to us, a matriarch of sorts," he answered at last. "Preparations begin when we receive a sign from her—no sooner. I can't say anything further."

"Then we'll stay," said Jupiter. He looked at me. "Won't we?"

I thought of my great uncle, who'd died years back. He was blind, with a hobbling gate, and every morning his daughter led him to the village square, where he sat on a stool all day, saying nothing, seeing nothing. At midday, his daughter brought him a meal, fed him, and went back to her chores. Then dusk came and his daughter walked him home again. My mother once told me that the man's daughter would be rewarded in the afterlife. "You, on the other hand," she said, "will probably shove me in the river when I get too old."

"Yes, we'll stay," I said. Brother Theos nodded once.

"Someone will alert you when the labor begins. You'll both be needed," said Brother Theos.

While we waited for the goat to go into labor, I wandered the streets of the monastery. The buildings were well-constructed, mostly of stone similar in color to the surrounding landscape. The church and other important buildings were made from a type of rock I'd never seen before. Whereas the surrounding mountains were dun-colored, this unfamiliar rock was white, with streaks of pale green.

Late one afternoon, the messenger came for us. He led us to a part of the monastery I hadn't come across before: a field of sorts, except that it was mostly bare of vegetation, aside from some twisted shrubs and the usual mountain grasses, which several of the monks' domesticated goats were chewing on noisily. The field was fenced on all sides, and in its center there was a large stone building. The building was made of the white and green stone, and it looked out of keeping with the otherwise rustic surroundings.

We followed the messenger into this building. It was round stable of sorts, with stalls along the perimeter and a raised platform in the middle. We found Brother Theos and another monk in one of the stalls. Theos huddled over a gray goat.

"It's as we feared," said Brother Theos when he saw us. "Stillborns."

He gestured toward floor of the stall. I moved closer. Two tiny bodies, still wet with their mother's fluids, lay in the grass that covered the packed earth floor. One was a goat, its body perfectly formed, but much too small. The other was not a goat, but the infant form of the goat men, its tiny animal head joined to a human infant's arms and torso. Its penis was small and hairless, like a human's, but below that its legs were that of a goat's: furred and hooved.

"The mother, I think, will give milk," said Theos, "but we'll need to tend to her for the next hours, to stimulate her teats. It's best, I think, for her to encounter you two now. She's not used to humans, but new mothers are suggestible. If you bond with her now she may accept you as the kids she's lost."

◇—

Once Jupiter and I finished the last of the unfortunate traveler's rations, we had nothing but goat's milk and greens as we waited for the mysterious divination rites to begin. We milked our goat several times a day, because Theos told us that frequent milking would encourage her to produce more.

I tried to make myself useful, but there were few places in the monastery where I was welcome. Jupiter had more luck—they let him work in the kitchens. I couldn't understand what work there was to do there, since the monks ate nothing but grass.

"Washing," said Jupiter, "and special meals for monks who are elderly or infirm." I inquired about helping with the infant goat-boys, but Theos told me that they were cared for by the mother goats during their earliest days. Their infancy was short—they developed at a pace more similar to goat kids than human children. Besides, it wasn't the birthing season.

Again a postulant came for us, shortly after we'd returned from dinner one night. "Brother Theos is ready to begin the divination rite," said the postulant. He fell silent. We got up, ready to follow him, but he waved one hand in protest.

"What is it?" I said. He gestured furiously, but neither Jupiter or I could understand, and he finally spoke again.

"You stay here," he said. "Only your brother comes."

Jupiter returned four or five hours later. He sat on the edge of his bed with his head in his hands.

"What happened?" I said.

"They brought me back to the birthing stables—you know, where we milked our goat the first time," he said. "It didn't—it didn't look the way it usually does."

He trailed off, as if at a loss, then continued, "They had the special nanny there, the one Brother Theos told us about. They call her Mother Genesis. She's very old, they said."

"What are you talking about?" Once again Jupiter was proving himself worthless.

"Brother Theos said that she's special. He said that she was born to the body of a female goat but possessed of a higher mind. She's older than any of them."

"But what did they do?" I said, impatient now. "What did they say about the village?"

"They said to make her pregnant," he said.

"The old nanny goat?" I said. My mind began to race. "What did you do?" I ventured.

"I didn't do anything," he said.

"That would be impossible," I said. "For a man to—"

"Stop," he said suddenly. "Stop talking."

I lay down again, and there was such a long silence that I thought he'd fallen asleep. Then he said, "Can't you ever be quiet?"

⊡

The next day another messenger came, again requesting only my brother. Jupiter returned to the room fifteen minutes later. He looked troubled.

"The preparation ceremony was successful," he said.

"What does that mean?" I asked. Jupiter didn't answer, but I thought I knew. He'd lied to me the night before. He'd done some nightmare thing with the old nanny goat. I could speculate no further, but I sensed some indecent, lurking logic—the secret rules by which the world became.

℔

Now we were waiting on Mother Genesis's mysterious gestation. Theos was vague about the details. In particular, he was annoyed by any attempt I made to find out how long the pregnancy would take. Jupiter was shifty, too, and I didn't dare broach the subject of what sort of creature was growing in Mother Genesis's womb.

I thought about the village sometimes. I didn't know how long they'd be able to ration the grain stored in the communal silo, but surely they were afraid by now, although it was difficult to imagine. In the same way that it would have been impossible for me to picture the monastery while I was still in the village, my memories of the village had taken on a certain unreality. I could picture the early mornings, when I washed my face and then filled the water jug in the river, but even so, I might have thought it was only a dream if Jupiter weren't here with me at the monastery.

One mild night, Theos himself, flanked by various assistants, arrived at our door just as we were drifting to sleep.

"It's time," said Theos.

"I'm coming, too, this time," I said. Theos ignored me. Jupiter looked muddled from sleep, but he rubbed his eyes and got out of bed. I followed them to the birthing stable. At the entrance to the stable, Theos stopped and turned to me.

"This rite is forbidden to you," he said.

I opened my mouth to argue, but I was unnerved by the look in his yellow eyes. Unusually, Theos seemed to expect a response from me.

"I'll wait outside," I said. Theos nodded and went on. The others followed, leaving me alone in the field.

For hours, nothing happened. I went and got a blanket from my room, and then returned and sat on the ground by some of the goats. Deep in the early hours of morning came the first sign of activity inside the stable: the monks were chanting.

It was cold, and I wrapped the wool blanket more tightly around myself. At the far corner of the pen, the goats huddled together. The moon shone brightly on the mass of humped woolen backs. The chants drifted eerily through the thin mountain air; the goats did not seem disturbed by the noise. I went over and lay next to them, and, comforted by their warmth, fell asleep.

♉

My head ached. Slowly I rolled over in the dirt and sat up. The birthing stable was quiet and still. From the look of the light, it was just past dawn, which on a usual day meant the monks were headed to the second prayer service of the day.

I pressed my ear to the wall of the stable. There was no sound, nor any sign of Theos or my brother. I walked back to our room. Jupiter was not in bed. Aimlessly, I wandered the streets, wondering where my brother was, until I spotted Jupiter and Theos outside the church, deep in conversation. They stopped talking when they saw me.

"I've been waiting for news," I said.

"The birthing ceremony was successful," said Theos. "We've divined the fate of your village."

"And?" I said.

My brother did not meet my eyes.

"Everyone from the village will die, if they are not dead already," said Theos. "But—but you can't possibly know that," I said. "How can you know?"

"The divination rite is not your concern," said Theos.

"There must be something, some offering we can make," I argued. "The village is faithful to the old ceremonies—"

"As I've already said, no one from the village will survive. Naturally, you feel concern. But there is nothing to be done."

"What about your goats?" I said. "Even if you gave us just one to bring back—"

"There's not enough milk to feed your village. Besides, your villagers are already starving. They'd slaughter any goat for her meat, and her unborn kids also. As you have seen, our own sons live in those wombs alongside their sisters. We do not send our children to slaughter."

"But what will we do?" I said.

"What you do now is none of our concern. Our obligations to prophecize and advise are fulfilled. Now you must leave the monastery."

"So you'd have us starve to death," I said angrily.

"It's not my caprice that determined your path. I didn't eat your grain. I didn't send the locusts. As I said, you'll have to depart from the monastery."

"Fine!" I said. "We'll go!"

"You misunderstand me," said Theos. "Your brother remains here. You alone must leave."

"What?" I said. I turned to Jupiter. Still he didn't meet my eye.

"We have no place for women," said Theos.

"I'm not a woman yet," I argued.

He waved his hand dismissively. "Only because you're close to starvation. If you were to stay here, drinking our milk, your menstruation would begin soon enough."

"No point in arguing," muttered Jupiter without looking up.

"Let us go to my office," said Theos to Jupiter. "There's more to discuss."

Of course Jupiter would stay here and let me starve because some half-human freak had told him that was how it had to be.

I waited until I felt sure that Theos would have finished with

Jupiter. Then I knocked on the office door.

"You want to question me further," he said when he saw who it was.

"Why are you letting my brother stay?" I demanded.

"He can be initiated into the Brotherhood."

"Then you lied. You said that no one from our village would survive," I said. He surveyed me with faint interest.

"You're more observant than your brother," he said. "Yes, I did say that none from your village survive. If your brother remains here, his body will remain human, but his soul will become something else. The man you know as your brother will not survive."

"He'll have a soul like yours?" I said.

"Perhaps," Theos shrugged. "He'll undergo a deep transformation, one that has not been attempted in many years. There's no way to know the outcome."

"But you know the outcome of my village."

"In that case, there is no uncertainty," he said. "There might have been a time when the destruction could have been avoided, but if there ever were such a time, it has passed. Now the consequences will follow one after another, in the same way a rockslide can't be stopped once it's begun. Your fool of a silo-keeper opened the silo to check the store while there were still locusts in the air. He didn't know it, but some insects laid their eggs inside. When your people discover their mistake they'll turn on each other. First they'll eat the pigs; then the rats and birds; then the grass. Then they'll dig worms from the ground. At last they'll eat each other. After that death will come swiftly."

"You can at least take in the men from my village. I'll bring them," I said. "You can transform them like my brother."

He considered me. "The stillborn kid that the Mother Genesis birthed last night is flesh from your brother's flesh. According to our laws it belongs, rightfully, to him. We have salted the meat and left it to dry in the sun. Its consumption is a requisite part of his transformation. But your brother is the only one with a rightful claim to such flesh."

"What about me? It's my kin, too," I said.

"As I've already said, you are soon a woman. You can't partake."

"So what am I supposed to do?"

Theos shrugged. "Do what you will."

When I returned to our bedroom, my brother was asleep in his bed, curled like a newborn. I shouldered my bag and quiver, put on my shoes, and picked up my bow. Then I sat on his bed and shook him awake gently.

"There's no point in waiting," I said.

"I've been thinking," he said. "Maybe there's some other way."

"I talked to Theos," I said. "There are no other possibilities. But don't be worried for me. I don't know if I believe him anyway. He's a freak of nature, some half-breed, not a god." Jupiter nodded.

"Get up and see me off," I said.

He rubbed his eyes and climbed from the bed. We emerged from the structure into bright afternoon sun. Across the plaza, the brothers had gathered to shear the nanny goats. As my brother crossed the plaza, I watched the sun glinting in the brown curls that covered the back of his head.

Then my arrow found its mark at the base of Jupiter's skull. He fell forward. I crossed the plaza and snapped the arrow protruding from his neck, so that I could roll him flat on his back. With one foot on his chest, I shot the second arrow into his throat. Just to be sure, I took out my knife and drove it hard into his chest.

The monk nearest me hurried to retrieve his pile of raw wool from the ground, so that it would not be soiled by the puddle of Jupiter's blood now seeping across the plaza. Brother Theos emerged from the crowd of shuffling goat-men and surveyed my brother's body impassively. "I'll need salt for the meat," I said.

Theos nodded.

IV. Exposition mode ended and I woke from the story as if from a nightmare. Dex and I were back at the table, across from the Salvo Salvation. The sunlight in the forest seemed just as gentle, just as newly minted. I felt my body, my real self, trembling violently in some far-off cubicle. This is an illusion, I told myself, but the Salvo Salvation, the girl who'd eaten her brother, was sitting right there, across from me. What sort of game was this?

I looked at my hands and tried to remember the granular detail of real-life vision. In real life the planes of my fingers met in perfect curves, without corners or visible edges. In real life, the backs of my hands were finely haired.

The Salvo Salvation smiled. "Let's eat, shall we?" she said. "Since you're the guests of honor, what would you like to eat?"

Dex watched her inscrutably from behind their black veil, their eyes approximating emotion too crudely for me to guess what he was feeling. Their white script appeared at the bottom of my visual field: "I want bread."

The Salvo Salvation smiled again. On Dex's plate appeared a loaf of bread, and beside it, a long serrated bread knife .

"Go ahead," she said.

Dex did not touch the bread knife but instead pulled one of their own knives from under their veil and swung it into the bread. All around us echoed a scream of pain, and then a keening sob. I looked instinctively to the woods, but in the bright soft sunlight there was no one.

Dex pulled out the knife. The inside of the bread was pulsating red flesh. Blood flowed from the cut Dex had made, more blood than was possible, puddling on the white dinner plate.

Dex's words appeared at the bottom of my visual field: "This isn't bread." "Of course it is," said the Salvo Salvation.

"Dex," I whispered, "Just eat it. It's a game; it's only a game."

Dex stood up suddenly. His chair fell backwards onto the grass.

"You can't leave in the middle of our meal," said the Salvo Salvation. As if there'd been a glitch in the graphics, the moment I had just seen reversed and replayed: the chair flew upright and Dex was seated; then, exactly as they had the first time, Dex shoved themself up from the table and the chair fell backward again. The moment looped faster and faster Dex's figure was a blur, expanding and contracting.

All at once, it stopped. Dex sat beside me as if they'd never stood up at all.

"I can't stand rude people," said the Salvo Salvation. She turned to me. "What would you like to eat?"

I'd seen a man beaten before. It didn't horrify me as much as I hoped it would. After a while the face didn't look like a face anymore. Without thinking, I looked at the Salvo Salvation and said, "Brussel sprouts." A pile of boiled brussel sprouts appeared on my plate.

"Don't stand on ceremony," said the Salvo Salvation.

I picked up the fork and poked at the brussel sprouts. I knew there would be flesh on the inside, but for now they looked exactly like brussel sprouts, horrible and slimy as the ones I'd eaten as a kid.

I peeled back one of the loose outer leaves of a brussel sprout. Behind the leaf a dark eye stared. They were eyeballs. I closed my eyes briefly. They weren't eyeballs; they weren't even brussel sprouts; they were only images.

Make it quick, I thought. The knife was sharper than any knife I'd used before and it cut the eyeball in half with hardly any effort. A brief scream rang in my ears. I cut again, then speared the small, gelatinous morsel on my fork. I put it in my mouth and held it on my tongue as the gag reflex came and went. It tasted of nothing. I swallowed.

The Salvo Salvation watched me, her eyes appraising. I set down my knife and fork. Then I said, "Dinner has been wonderful, but I think we have to go now."

"Your friend hasn't eaten yet," she said.

"Dex isn't hungry," I said quickly.

"After such a long journey? I don't believe it. You're only trying to save my feelings. You don't like the food, do you?" she said.

Dex sat silently, arms hanging at their side, fists clenched.

"They don't eat meat," I said.

"We haven't gotten to the meat course yet," said the Salvo Salvation. "Tell them to hurry up and finish their bread. Everyone is waiting on them."

I glanced at Dex again. They had to begun to rock slightly in place.

"What about you?" said the Salvo Salvation to me. "Do you eat meat?"

"Yes," I said. I tried to smile at her.

"Which kind is your favorite?"

"I don't know. All kinds. I mean," I fumbled, "most kinds."

"Poultry?" she said.

"Sure. Poultry," I said.

"Well, if your friend refuses to eat," she said to me, "then we'll have to move onto the next course without them, don't you think?" She studied her fingernails.

Dex looked over at me.

"It's a game, Dex, do you understand?" I whispered to them. "Me, you, her, we're playing a game. Your body—your real self—you're far away. Dex isn't even your real name, is it? Where are you housed? Iowa City? Tell me, Dex, please tell me where you really are."

The Salvo Salvation looked up. She said, "I asked if you thought we should move on. Apparently you don't have an opinion."

Suddenly Dex's looming veiled figure disappeared from the chair. In its place was a turkey, and atop its awkward feathered neck sat Dex's head in miniature, his face unveiled, black eyes blinking in the sunlight, inscrutable.

"Dex!" I said.

"Turkey?" offered the Salvo Salvation.

"No," I said, "No."

"You prefer chicken," she said. Dex's lanky, naked body appeared, their neck fading into a monstrous black-eyed rooster's head.

"Please, no, I don't like it."

"You're a picky eater," scolded the Salvo Salvation.

"Where is Dex?"

"Your friend didn't want to partake."

"Where are they? What did you do to them?" I said.

"Finish your food," she ordered.

Dex's chair was empty again. On a tray in front of me splayed the body of a small roast chicken, lying face down. Below its wings the body narrowed into a slim waist, a human waist, and stretching from the waist were Dex's legs in miniature, laid flat over a long porcelain tray.

"Leg?" she said.

"Wings," I said, "I prefer wings."

A bone cracked as she pulled a crisp wing from the body and

laid it on my plate. With trembling hands I cut the steaming meat and
ate.

Ψ

V. Then I was back in the desert, at the end of the road, or else
its beginning. The road was dark and ordinary. "Dex?" I called. The
words appeared in my field large white print, as if someone else had said
them. I checked my map. The red star marking Dex's location was
absent.

I stepped onto the road. The perpetual sunset had found time,
and it dimmed as I walked toward it, just like sunsets are supposed to. I
heard nothing but a soft scratching of an electric lizard scuttling across
the sand somewhere just out of sight. Then the light of the sun had
gone.

A pale moon rose wrongly in the west. I felt a drop of rain on
my arm, and then another, and then all at once it was pouring. I kept
walking.

The rain was relentless. Already a half-inch of water covered
the road. Small lights flickered across the surface of the rising flood: the
electric lizards were swimming. I had always wondered why they had
webbed feet. Now I saw that everything must have happened before,
and like all animals they'd been waiting for it to happen again.

The static age ends and reality jerks once, twice, green and gold and glittering, and then cyberspace gives way to meatspace again, the inside of your eyelids tuned to a dead tv channel as the neuromancy ends and we again are sipping tea.

You look down at the jar of jam, but do not touch the knife.

"Do you know the thing about figs and wasps?" I ask, topping another cracker, my appetite perfectly intact.

"I know Jesus cursed a fig tree," you offer.

"Fig wasps," I say, "are a pollinator, and in the wild fig trees are completely dependent upon them for reproduction, and vice versa. The immature female flower inside the fruit releases a scent that attracts the female wasps, and they crawl inside of the fig. The opening is so tight that oftentimes the wasp loses an antenna, or their wings. It doesn't matter, though. It's a one way trip, so they just keep pushing, pushing, pushing. Once inside, they lay their eggs inside the seeds, and then they die, the dead body nourishing the fruit and the juvenile insects crawl out and fly off to pollinate the next tree."

You look again at the jam on the table, catching the candlelight.

"Of course, most commercial figs these days use a more refined process." I walk to a drawer near the stove, opening it and rummaging inside. "For this next bit, I'll need your cooperation and participation."

Looking at me expectantly, I raise a smooth white mask, a black diamond under each eye.

You nod, and I softly slip the mask over your face, and when you peer out through the eye holes, the world is paper again. "To mask, to hide the truth... that's the idea, anyway. But perhaps it is more complicated; perhaps sometimes flesh is the real liar, and the plaster shell the revealer of truth. Think on it as you..."

BLEED FOR YOUR WISHES

R.S. Saha

ᛏ

Lorn left the building, tugging the door shut behind her. She blinked and squinted against the sunlight before pulling her hoodie up to hide the hideous haircut she had been given. A section above her right ear still wept blood from Mother's scissors cutting too wildly.

The air was suffocating. It dehydrated Lorn with every breath. Together with the sun's brightness, she trudged under the burden of yet another disconnect. She felt very wet on the inside. She had been arguing with Mother from early morning to noon. Yelling. Unleashing the storm running rampant inside her. Calm, soothing words that fell like a drizzle had no effect on convincing Mother of the truth. Lorn had opted for anger instead. Screaming and demanding that Mother listen.

It hadn't worked. And Lorn, afraid of her own strength, gave in to Mother's demands. Of the two women, one of them had the strength of testosterone. That one was very afraid of the harm she could do.

So Lorn, throat raw, dragged her feet as she walked; a castaway on a desert island that was determined to push her back into stormy waves. She bent her head against its demands and kept moving. No particular direction. Just not towards home. Taking whichever turn took her away from larger crowds. Looking everywhere but reflective surfaces—like the eyes of people. She stopped only when she had to, when the fear of unintended consequences overwhelmed the urge to walk into traffic.

The burning of her calves and the cramping of her feet eventually got through to her and she realized she had been wandering for hours. Every muscle in her body was tense and flexed like a boxer's arm at the moment of impact. Her head spun and she sagged in a dark corner, eyes darting around for somewhere to eat.

She spotted a restaurant across the street in a place she thought she had already looked. Stairs rose to a squat brick building set farther away from the street than the towering, concrete edifices astride it. The restaurant had a bay window to the right of its stairs and the left had a vertically aligned sign that read: The Votive.

Warm, orange light glowed through the bay window's curtains like a campfire. The place looked expensive but Lorn was too hungry to keep looking for something else. She crossed the empty street, shivered as she entered the shadows of the buildings on the other side, and climbed the stairs. She slid her hand up the cool metal railing, appreciating that it wasn't chipped or rusted like most of the city's rails. On reaching the landing, she saw that the sign was made of wood and the letters had been burned in.

Lorn entered through the door and found herself in a small waiting room with a hallway in front of her leading into the restaurant. The entire space was suffused with a soft, dim orange light. To her left, there were three high-backed, muslin chairs lined up against the pine green wallpaper. To the right, two of the walls were covered in paintings of various forest scenes. Lorn stepped closer to look at them and saw people running and playing among the trees. Their faces were stretched in expressions of rapture and pain. All of them had scarlet pits where eyes should have been. Lorn swallowed hard and turned away from the paintings to look at the third wall, the one bordering the street. It had a wide shelf, from floor to ceiling, crammed full of leather bound books. Lorn reached a hand for a random one, drawn by the gold petals on its spine.

"Welcome to The Votive."

Lorn cried out and turned.

There was someone with long black hair in the hallway. They stood with their gloved hands clasped in front of their waist. Their brown face was round and youthful with sharp features. They smiled, their full lips remaining closed. They were wearing a gold name tag on their black silk waistcoat that was unreadable in the dim lighting. "I am the Host."

"Hi," Lorn stammered.

Their smile widened. "May we have your name?"

She reflexively told them what she always told strangers. The name she still held onto, afraid of the change. Afraid she was wrong and Mother was right.

The storm inside Lorn that had calmed to a downpour, settled down to a drizzle.

"It is done," the Host said solemnly. Then they frowned, cocking their head to their right, and temporarily revealing an ear. "Hmm. Interesting. Tell me your name."

Lorn hesitated, wondering if the Host's ear really was pointy. She told herself she was seeing things and answered again without repeating herself. "Lorn."

The Host nodded and motioned with their hand for Lorn to follow.

The hallway had the same pine green wallpaper and had no light of its own, instead being lit by the waiting room and the main room of the restaurant. The wooden floor beneath them creaked with each of Lorn's steps, growing more and more noticeable every second. The hallway seemed to grow narrower and Lorn's heart beat its way up to her throat. The hallway squeezed to a chokepoint in the middle, in the darkest point, and Lorn almost turned and ran out. She was compelled to continue anyway. The creaks broke past the stringed instruments playing in the main room: long, mournfully drawn out progressions interrupted by moaning wood and the raucous beating of her heart. It was like her heart was roaring at her to leave.

They entered the main room and her heart rate returned to normal. Lorn couldn't see any instruments or even speakers but the music continued.

The room was wider than it was deep, with a vaulted ceiling arching up to shadowed reaches. Three chandeliers, crystals burning bright, hung over the sole table in the room. The table and its chairs were made of dark brown wood. A dark blue table runner was the only thing on its surface. Beyond the table was a massive marble fireplace. It dominated the wall, making the entire center portion of the table its hearth. Its mantle, glowing with flickering orange light, was carved with a myriad of animals both real and mythical. In the middle, the very middle, a cherubic face smiled directly down at the floor, away from the room. Its downturned features cast sinister shadows on itself.

"As a special guest," the Host said, "you may sit within our hearth's grace. Would you like to face it or have your back to it?"

"Facing it," Lorn said. She didn't like the idea of having her back to the demonic cherub. "What do you mean *special* guest?"

The Host pulled a chair out for Lorn. "We have taken an interest in you."

Lorn hesitated. "We?"

"Yes," the Host said. "Please sit, Lorn."

She was drawn by the quiet request, but she also felt like she should turn and leave. Lorn frowned at the thought. *'Should' leave? Why not 'could' leave?*

"Please sit," the Host repeated. "*Lorn.*"

The Host's voice rang clear as a bell and had the rough, rustling quality of a dry leaf. It had autumn's allure.

Lorn sat down without hesitation and allowed the Host to push the chair in. She wondered if her voice would ever be pretty like theirs.

"The Manager will be with you shortly."

"I didn't ask to see…" Lorn turned. "Oh."

The Host was already walking away.

Lorn shifted in her seat, toes curling and relaxing in her shoes. There were no other tables in the room. Maybe it was meant to be a communal experience. Two other people were at the table, both on the hearth side and both in the darker areas of the table. Half their features glowed bright from the fire and the other half was cast in shadow. Neither were eating.

One of them was slumped in his chair, skin gaunt and sweaty. He coughed into a handkerchief every few seconds. Lorn nodded at both of the other guests in greeting and they both looked away. She shrank in her seat.

"You are an interesting one," a husky voice said from behind. "Lorn."

The voice's owner partially sat on the table to Lorn's left. Lorn half smiled. "H-hello."

"I am the Manager," she said. Her black, oiled hair flowed in thick curls down to her chest. Her beautiful brown face was also round and youthful, like the Host, but her features were softer. A flat nose, chubby cheeks, and full lips. Her black eyes glowed like charcoal in a fire.

Lorn squeezed her chair's arms. A fog was settling in her mind, diffusing thoughts before they could find cohesion.

"You may have noticed that there is no menu."

Lorn nodded. She couldn't make herself any smaller. The Manager's kohl-lined eyes made her wonder if she needed to. It would be okay. She was a *special* guest, after all.

"We fulfill a different kind of hunger at this table," the Manager continued. "In exchange for something precious, we fulfill wishes." The Manager's lips finally parted in a smile, revealing canines that were pointed like fangs.

"Consider our surprise when you arrived with *two* precious… identities," the Manager said. She spoke slowly, like every word was a stranger to her mouth. She sighed and adjusted her red sari to cover more of her stomach. The gold bangles on her wrists chimed against each other. "Of course you gave us the one that was less valuable to you. And therefore less valuable to us. However, you still thought of it as yours. No matter how little. That's what matters. That's what we need," she paused, frowning to herself. "No, no. Not need. Want. We give *you* what *you* want by taking what *you* need and *we* want. Understand?"

"No," Lorn rasped. "Ma'am."

"Oh my, what a… dry, deep voice for a beautiful woman." The Manager held Lorn's chin with a warm hand and moved Lorn's face from side to side, studying it. "Such… amateurish attempts to bring out the truth. Ah well. Humans cannot be blamed. And you, Lorn, have only just started the process. These things take an inordinate amount of time for your… kind."

The Manager straightened and stopped smiling. Her amused expression remained, similar to how hungry, arrogant men leered at impressionable girls.

A predator's amusement.

"It will be painful," the Manager said. "But you will leave happier than the other guests—the poor fools. You will be getting a need *and* a want, essentially for free. The Owner was quite delighted by your cleverness, you see. As unintended as it was." She looked at the two others at the table. They didn't seem to have noticed her. "Them however… ah, well. The exchange has been made. They must live on with it."

Lorn found her voice and some clarity, though the fog still remained in her mind. "Live with what? What's happening here?"

The Manager was gone.

"Hello?" Lorn stretched around in her seat, straining her neck to look behind her chair. "Hello…" Lorn frowned. What was she doing? Who was she looking for?

She sat normally and began tapping the arm of her chair. The music became more discordant like the conductor had lost control of their musicians. It echoed and creaked. Strings screeched. Sections played over and over and over again, stuck in a repetitious loop, until they suddenly moved on. Each played at different speeds, anywhere from slow enough to seem like the instrument had stopped playing to fast enough to become a high frequency fever pitch.

Lorn heard none of it. Frozen in place, she was deafened by the sight in front of her.

One of the guests—a man judging by the name and wish spoken by the cherub shortly before the horror started—was hanging in the air. A black noose had dropped from the darkness, wrapped around his neck, and tugged back up into the ceiling until he was hanging a few feet above his chair. The short man flailed wildly. His fingers dug into the black rope tightening around his neck. His nails broke from the effort and began to bleed, red runnels streaming down the back of his hand and hairy arms. He was still breathing, gasping for lungfuls of air every second.

Two ropes snaked out from under the table and circled around his legs. They began pulling until the silent creaking of his bones turned into snapping and popping. He began screaming now, between gulps of air. He screeched, grating on his throat and vocal cords enough to have surely shredded them into a salty and bloody pulp.

He was silenced when a dark gray hood descended over him but his screams weren't stopped. They still made him shake his head from side to side. The hood molded around him like shrinkwrap and smudged his features. Shallow dips for eyes, a mound for his nose, and a moist circle for his mouth.

The cherub said the next name and then that name's wish to be cured. The other guest, the sick man, yelped as vines tied around his wrists. He was lifted up into the air with his arms spread like he was going to be crucified. He began coughing excessively, stomach heaving in between bouts and face twisted in pain. He tugged at the vines and kicked in the air. His lips formed the words *let me go* without any sound coming out. His pallored skin shimmered with sweat.

Four ropes with hooked ends appeared, writhing like snakes. They impaled the man's back—two on the left and two on the right—and pulled. The ropes went taut as skin and flesh were peeled back like wings. More blood rained down onto the table as the man's ribs were broken and spread in a similar manner. He had stopped trying to beg for escape and only screamed and coughed amidst the cracking of his bones.

He was given a third set of wings in the form of his opened and spread lungs. More vines appeared now, thin as thread with small green hands on the ends. Slender fingers dug into the man's open lungs and lifted away clutching bleeding masses of dark flesh. They returned clean and empty moments later and dug for more. Again and again.

His coughing grew intermittent.

The cherub on the mantle looked at Lorn and smiled. It spoke the first name Lorn had said; the one she had *given*.

Lorn tried to get up. Her legs gave out under her and she collapsed into her chair.

The cherub on the mantle stated Lorn's need.

The fire burst from the fireplace like a dragon's breath, arched over the table, and engulfed her. It burned away the baggy clothes that hid her body from herself and the world. It burned away what little hair remained on her scalp.

When Lorn howled, hunched over to be as small as possible, two stakes thrust through her back and out her pecs. Blood lit by firelight oozed onto the stubble on her chest, hissing into smoke. The flames burned away her chest hair as the stakes retracted. The burning sensation came from inside now as muscles and bone structure began to change inside Lorn. It spread within like a wildfire, melting and reshaping muscle; altering and forging bone; creating fat where there was none before.

No more. Please. Lorn begged internally. A mask was being molded onto her face, blinding and suffocating her. *I can't take this. Please. No more.*

"An accord has been made," the Manager said, her voice flowering in Lorn's mind. "It must be seen through. The Owner demands it."

The Manager's voice withered into nothing. Vines with hands similar to the ones digging in the second guest appeared through the flames. Lorn did not see the sharp talons the hands had but she felt them dig into her scalp. Were it not for the mask on her face, Lorn would have been the first to see her new luscious black hair as it sprouted from her head and fell around her face like a shroud.

Instead, the first to see it was the first guest. He had been set down on his feet by the noose. He was now taller than before and had conventionally handsome features unmarred by unfair genetics. He thought about waiting for the woman in front of him to be set free so he could talk to her. The thought didn't remain long. It didn't even return when he noticed her bare breasts. The realization made him frown.

The frown also abandoned him.

With a disinterested sigh and shrug, the hollowed and handsome man left the silent main room.

The fire burned away Lorn's mask and chair. She fell into the pile of ashes and spat as some of it got in her mouth. She groaned and got to her feet on shaking legs. The ash came with her, flowing up her bare body like waves on a shore. The ash meshed together and began shimmering like starlight. In seconds, Lorn was wearing a foam white sundress.

She noticed a man staring at her. He was holding a handkerchief. She smiled at him, her dark brown eyes looking right into his. "Hello."

His eyes came into focus for a moment upon hearing a voice like summer. His gaze rapidly grew distant again. He grunted unintelligibly and turned to leave. He dropped his handkerchief as he did so.

Lorn picked it up and sped after him down the short hallway. She caught up to him at the door. "Sir? You dropped this."

"Mmm?" He turned. "Oh. That. No…no I won't be needing it."

"Huh?"

"I won't," he mumbled and left the restaurant. "No, no."

"I can dispose of that for you."

"Ah!" Lorn yelped, flinching away from the Host. "You scared me!"

"Apologies, Lorn." The Host took the handkerchief from her. "Did you enjoy your meal?"

"Yeah! The veggie burger was really good. I'll have to bring my friends here."

The Host smiled. "Please do. The Owner would like that."

"Bye," Lorn said cheerfully.

She stepped out into the city and took a deep breath. The restaurant smelled delicious but fresh air was unmatched. She waved a cab down.

"Where to, ma'am?" the driver asked.

Lorn gave the address that always came first to her mind.

The cab slowly maneuvered back onto the busy street. Lorn relaxed with her hands on her lap and her head against the window. A small smile grew on her face under the light of the sun. Breathing soft and slow, Lorn watched the city and its people pass by. Lorn's smile widened on the rare occasion someone looked into the cab and saw her. Then it would shrink as the cab drove on.

She smiled in that joyful and pleasant manner all the way to Mother's house.

⚴

Your hands reach up and remove the mask, and as you turn it over and look down into its empty eyes, you see that the previously nondescript face has shifted into a simulacra of your own, and you set it down on the formica before looking back up at me expectantly.

"We're almost there," you say, and there it is in your voice—that tinge of melancholy that always comes when a parting of ways is about to occur or the party is about to run out of nitrous.

"There?" I ask. "Darling, we've been there the whole time. There's only journey. Surely you understand that by now?"

Again I refill both of our mugs, and we allow ourselves to share a moment of silence, our Foolish trek down the road paused for a minute just to savor the dust beneath our boots and the warm smell of colitas rising up through the air.

Something that is not quite a frown tugs at your lips, and something that is not quite my familiar easy smile answers.

"Will I remember?" you ask. "When it's all over?"

"When the scene shifts, you mean?"

You nod.

"That's out of my hands," I say, and I go to another cupboard, and when this one opens you see a variety of knick knacks and bric-a-brac, Beanie Babies *and stuffed clowns and dolls of all sorts and shapes and professions.*

Cautious fingers remove one particular ornament, a penny doll that has been glued to the top of a music box, the two almost certainly not paired together originally. The box is stained a rosy mahogany, and I set it in front of you, winding the knob.

The little face of the porcelain girl looks at you with blank eyes as a tinkling rendition of Andrew Lloyd Webber's "Memories" begins to play, and my voice joins the music: "Little lives, caught in china, characters conjured by characters, porcelain and paper... Oh, to be a doll, to be played with and treasured and taken care of... trapped by perfection, forevermore a..."

FROZEN CHARLOTTE

Mildred Faintly

From the Casebook of Doctor Coppelius

The patient A. was a man in his thirties, unmarried, a minor official in the local government here in Vienna; eminently respectable, enjoying the esteem of his colleagues and the confidence of his superiors. His parents and siblings were persons of the most prosaic normalcy, presenting no genetic cause for A.'s condition. Superficially, A. appeared quite ordinary, except in his care for his physical appearance, which at times approached nattiness. A. came to me suffering from the usual constellation of neurasthenic symptoms, ennui and spleen and a number of other related italics — evidently the result of reading worldly (i. e., French, books), and exacerbated by the practice of onanism which was, as is common nowadays, greatly facilitated by Internet access. It soon became apparent that A.'s psyche had been early on tainted by unwholesome reflection (delectatio morosa), and a morbid interest in the by-ways of Classical literature, especially the monstrous rhetorical orchids one may cull from the late Latin poets Claudian and Dracontius.

These tendencies had been worsened by an early failure to participate whole-heartedly in team-sports. While undergoing treatment, his condition degenerated further in the direction of irrevocable metamorphosis sexus, accompanied by sensations of unreality. It is best to give the facts in his own words, as recorded in my notes: these are of course somewhat condensed, but the expressions are his own, and offer a valuable insight into the acquisition of a reversed sexual instinct, and what must denominate as an alteration in his state of being. Not his well being, but his being itself. Here I believe I may offer to psychiatry a record of something undiscovered. A bold claim, I know, to set before a profession already well acquainted with nearly "all the wonders that the hot sun hatches," to borrow Nietzsche's splendid phrase.

The tragic outcome of A.'s relentless obsessions, seems in retrospect a foregone conclusion. Hopefully this clinical record may permit a swifter recognition of the situation and save other unfortunates from the same fate. In the following account, I will alternate a condensed version of the patient's disclosures with my own comments, so that my colleagues in psychiatry may follow exactly the course of the treatment, and profit from my errors (alas!) as well as my insights.

W

A.'s Narrative

I received a traditional education of a sort nowadays uncommon since my parents, prospering during the boom postwar years, were able to send me to a school that had not fully emerged from the nineteenth century. There my character was formed, and perhaps deformed, by the sort of instruction that defined a gentleman in the days of the Austro-Hungarian Empire.

With the intellectual advantages secured by this excellent education, I was easily able to pass the examination to obtain a post in the civil service, which I still hold. I remained a bachelor, despite my best efforts at dating. Women considered me good company, and found me entertaining, but never seemed to regard me as a romantic prospect. On a number of occasions I pursued friendships with women, but these never advanced beyond the platonic. Inevitably the objects of my attentions would meet another man who would be chosen as a mate. Without exception it was a dull brute, innocent of literature, the sort who could placidly belch and scratch himself while demanding "What's was for dinner?" It became clear to me that I could never arrive at this level of simian masculinity, even with the mightiest backward effort of the mind. An unthinking state is not to be attained by thinking. I abandoned all hope of fulfilling the masculine role with a woman, and resigned myself to a celibate life. I continued my education, so long pursued in libraries, in adult bookstores.

This state of affairs continued until I came across a circular in Human Dressage, *one of the specialized periodicals to which I had become addicted. Therein a certain Madame Magda Wang offered initiation into the techniques of a highly specialized Taoist yoga, which would, she asserted, realign and center one's character, endow one with a new and existential certainty in all one's affairs.*

Her photograph showed a determined, even aggressive looking woman with a predatory sparkle in her eyes, which inspired confidence in the efficacy of her program of spiritual discipline. The description of her methods was more suggestive than informative, but she referred readers to her memoirs, The Purple Days, *published by the Institute of Anthroposophy. The volume was not cheap, but considering the rarity of the insights it promised, I considered the expense justifiable.*

At length the book arrived, and I was not disappointed by its contents. Born in Budapest to a Chinese-Austrian couple, Magda Wang passed her childhood in the Hong Kong where her father's presence was demanded by business interests. In a curious eccentricity, her father had taken her mother's name, Wang, at the time of their marriage.

The girl Magda grew up in that tiny British colony in East Asia, equally at ease in Chinese, German and English. The city had become a principal refuge for Taoist adepts when the communists proscribed religion on the mainland, and Magda took an interest in "The Way" in her teens, rapidly advancing on a mystical path which included not a few elements of what we in the West would call sorcery.

Her narrative recounted her sometimes hair-raising initiations into the upper levels of practice, and her encounters with various ghosts and spirits. Of particular interest was her cryptic description of Taoist erotic practices, which increase one's spiritual power by sublimating sexual energy. In keeping with Madame Wang's high decorum, these passages were allusive, taking the form of a commentary on the Tao Te Ching. Though there are countless translations of that inestimable anthology of mystical poetry, they are as rule not true translations but reworkings of earlier renderings. Even the fresh attempts by genuine Sinologists, like dear old Arthur Waley, rely on traditional, medieval Chinese commentaries, which explain away the book's genuine difficulties with pious platitudes. Though my own grasp of Chinese is amateur at best, I was able, dictionary in hand, to confirm that Madame Wang's interpretations did ample justice to the often inexplicable turns of phrase. One could say of her renderings, "the text here is cryptic, but if it means anything at all, it surely means this."

I was particularly struck by the lines:

One who knows the Dao's maleness
yet cherishes within himself its femaleness,
is a bond between heaven and earth,
a link between the masculine clarity of sky
and the patient yielding of the land.
The eternal power of the Dao never leaves him,
and he returns, comes home to a childlike state

He knows and shares in the glory, the splendor of the Dao,
he cherishes the shame and disgrace of it too.
He is the most perplexing being in heaven or earth,
no one understands why he accepts all that befalls him
as a valley accepts every stream.

I felt these lines limned the most secret contours of my soul. I saw in them the promise of somehow alchemizing the shame that accompanied my most private reveries into a confident acceptance of my entire existence. The verses spoke to me in ways I did not even wish to resist.

Doctor Coppelius's Comment

It should startle no one that Daoism, with its conscious idealization of the Yin, the feminine principle, would give the somewhat effeminate A. the sense that he intuitively understood, and was understood by, the text. The femininity of Chinese poetic culture is a subject that has never been adequately considered, nor is it likely to receive a fair and full treatment in the present political climate, though it was noted as long ago as the days of Wilde & Whistler.

More disquieting than the implied abdication of masculinity, is the retreat from independent existence implied by the phrase "in ways I did not even wish to resist." A persistent motif in A.'s self-disclosures was fatalism, the no longer reluctant "realization" that he is what he is for life, that he was born to be this and could have been nothing else.

A.'s Narrative

Madame Wang's circular in Human Dressage *noted that she was available for private instruction, and the post office box given for inquiries was right here in Vienna. I wrote to her in a frenzy of enthusiasm, not pausing to reflect on what I said for fear of losing my nerve. I stamped and sealed my letter and walked briskly to the nearest mailbox. I heard its metal entry clang shut upon my missive with a mixture of dread and relief, something like what a criminal must feel when the cell door clashes closed behind him. Fear of what may happen next, and a strange comfort at realizing the decisions are no longer his.*

After several months of cruel anticipation, when I'd frankly given up hope of receiving a response, there came a letter from Madga Wang, saying she'd been touched by the frank details of my history, and had confidence I was a good candidate for her spiritual guidance. She gave an address and an evening when she would receive me. There was no question of negotiation or scheduling. I would present myself then.

On the appointed evening I was at her door, several minutes early. As is my habit when paying calls, I stood at the door with my eyes on my watch, rapping the very second the appointed hour struck.

Madame Wang met me graciously, took my hat and coat, and led me into a parlor which was a veritable Wunderkammer, a private museum of ethnographic and natural history curiosities, antiquities and art objects. All of these were remarkable, from the Ptolemaic Osiris figure to the remarkably plausible Fiji mermaid with a diminutive 18th century powdered wig, tied in the back with a ribbon, on its wizened head. But they were surpassed by several china dolls in a magnificent miniature house.

China dolls have nothing to do with the country China: they were first produced a little to the north of here, in Germany, in the 1840's, and there the finest examples are still made. They are named for the porcelain from which heads are formed, like little portrait busts. The hair and facial features are painted and glazed, which gives them a glossy, and at times eerily realistic appearance, alive yet unalive. The slightly uncanny impression created by these figures is well attested by the name given to a particular and popular model: the "Frozen Charlotte." The name came from an American folk ballad, which described a young woman who would not wrap up warmly for a New Year's Eve sleigh ride because she didn't wish to hide her pretty dress from view. The ballad concludes,

How quickly into the lighted hall,
Her rigid form is borne.
They call her name, they chafe her hands,
Her life they'd fain restore,
but Charlotte is a frozen corpse,
she'll never answer more.

Three diminutive Charlottes stood in the drawing room of Madame Wang's doll house. They were, as the ballad would lead one to expect, of a chilling beauty. Their realism suggested the embalmer's art as much as the doll-maker's skill.

We sat on Madame Wang's couch. She poured me coffee and offered me a slice of sacher-torte. It was in some ways a stiffly traditional Viennese at-home even amid that jungle of oddities.

She asked whether I was able to commit to her program of spiritual development, to fully entrust myself to her direction? There would be no question of compensation. What she had to offer was "not for money and not for everyone."

She explained that manly independence and a strong sense of self would not be assets here. Spiritual progress depended on absolute submission to her tutelage: mine must be an unconditional surrender. Once I declared myself her pupil, if I should then hesitate or demur, she had methods (here she clenched her teeth) of strengthening my resolve.

As I gazed upon her strong determined features and took in the stylish leopard-print pattern of her riding-coat, I was overcome by her personal style as much as by her words, I pledged myself to her, come what may.

"What I will teach you," she said, is shwon pin. We must use the Chinese words because the concept itself doesn't fully exist in the West. The phrase comes from the sixth chapter of the Dao De Jing. Perhaps we could render it with Blake's phrase "the shadowy female," This is the name of the spirit of the feminine, the yielding yin quality that is the very heart of Taoist teaching. The Western words I could use to characterize yin — womanly, female, feminine; dark, cold, passive — mislead, because they only describe aspects. We must have recourse to the Chinese. The first character, shwon," (here she drew it on a piece of paper)

means "black, dark; profound, mysterious" and shows a piece of thread. The reasoning here is that thread is dyed, whence we go to the idea of darkness, of mystery. There is also the implication of something woven or knotted; from the idea of the knot we proceed to the notion of the difficult and mysterious.

"The next character, pin," (here she took up her pen once more,)

牝

meaning: "female; female animal; cow", shows on the left a cow's head with horns on top. This makes it clear we have to do with a physical, mammalian reality. On the right the character for man

人

inverted,

匕

The first little image shows a man standing up on his two legs. In the second, which is the form it takes in the word pin, his legs are in the air, and his upper body is bent round as if to look back at the height he'd fallen from. The use of the inverted man in the character indicates that the female is the opposite or complement of the male.

"But for us this character has a further, esoteric meaning. The reversed person is the emblem of transformation, like the "Hanged Man" of the Tarot deck. It represents the "death" which is part of true initiation: loss of self and a passing beyond the limits of mortal existence."

Doctor Coppelius's Comment

As a man whose world-view is determined by science, I was unable to credit the claims made by Madame Wang, and assumed that she simply victimized the unfortunate A. by exploiting the his Oedipal susceptibilities.

But it a poor sort of scientist who is never skeptical of his own skepticism, so I ask the reader to defer a dogmatic dismissal of Madame Wang's pretensions, and follow the case history with as open a mind as possible

Under Wang's direction, A. undertook a regimen of yogic exercises, particularly breathing meditation, aimed at strengthening his chee, a Chinese word which means, literally, "breath," but (like the Hebrew ruak, the Latin anima, and the Greek pneuma,) has along with this root meaning the connotation of spirit, soul or vital force. He adopted a diet which excluded meat, alcohol, and even grains.

Along with this he was subjected to a course of erotic training, which was characterized by sexual submission and denial of orgasm—the anxiety resulting from this frustration of libido of course found relief in the rest of the "spiritual regimen," which was in fact an artificially induced symptom, which at once expressed and relieved his psychic malaise. It had the same calming effect upon A. as the "rituals" of obsessive compulsives. All this confirmed him in his idolatrous devotion to the woman who now possessed him, almost in the demonic sense.

The details of A.'s activities can easily be imagined and need not be repeated here. Masochism is the most common of neuroses, and its particulars are as banal as they are well known. What was unusual was the pseudo-religious intensity which was imparted to them by Madame Wang's mystical claims, and which were accepted without reservation by the neuropathic and morbidly sensitive A.

Madame Wang's Journal

I remember my first interview with my Taoist master in Hong Kong. We sat in his run-down little apartment drinking tea; while he explained to me in wearisome detail some fine points regarding the I Ching. One of the light-bulbs in the fixture overhead expired with fizzle and pop, and we found ourselves conversing in a dreary 40 watt twilight, which made the shabbiness of the decor ever more dispiriting. I began to wonder whether this fellow wasn't another of the greedy frauds and third rate mediums who peddled amulets and promises to others as badly off as he. But then the master took a slip of yellow paper, drew on it the character for the moon along with a few lines of esoteric script, and stuck it high up on the wall. The abstracted crescent of the moon character glowed on the paper, and grew into a round, full and bright, though miniature, moon that shone down upon us from the wall which had melted into fog around it.

The room itself took on a luminous, hazy quality, and the cracked formica table became a fine teak example of the carpenter's and carver's art, the fragrance of the tea, now steaming in delicate porcelain cups, became rich and rare. The lesson continued in a lunar palace.

I came to understand two things that evening. That magic may be employed casually, but never without need. Our lunar excursion had been made for the sake of the light; the master was never concerned with whether I was impressed or not.

And this was also my introduction to the mechanics of Taoist magic, which, like the Tao Te Ching, comes into being at the beginning of the Common Era, with the Chinese discovery of how to make paper. To be sure, there had been mediumship, shamanism and no shortage of religions and philosophies before then, but the breakthrough to real esoteric science seems to have depended on paper. Previously, all writing had been done on long slats of bamboo sewn together like window-blinds, a manner of publication so cumbersome that the Analects of Confucius would have filled a small cart. Paper brought about an awareness that the characters had their own independent reality. They represented physical forms, but were independent of them. The nearly weightless medium which now carried the characters, and the simple flammability of paper, made it clear that what was written, which could at the touch of a flame pass over into the realm of immaterial, existed on an intermediate level of being between real and unreal. Figured and printed paper began to be used as joss offerings, for reflective minds saw how writing formed a permeable membrane between the levels of being.

Anyone who has been transported into a further world by reading a novel has experienced the occult potential of the written word. Reading a fantasy or science fiction short story is in fact an authentic religious experience. To be sure, not a particularly high level one, but the way in which such reading holds time in abeyance, and can distract from even such insistent physical reality as noise or bodily pain, makes it clear that reading literature is a kind of trance.

What the sorcerer does is enter far more more fully into the world of the written. This is most effectively achieved in Chinese or Ancient Egyptian, since these are the only fully developed writing systems consisting of pictures. Western amulets, particularly Arabic ones, where the text is sometimes calligraphed into an image, show a faint awareness of how the work must be carried out. The Egyptians made perhaps a little too much progress in this direction: in their literature the quantity of spells outweighs every other literary genre.

Written Chinese is the most difficult of languages to learn, since it doesn't have any letters at all. Egyptian had a set of alphabetic characters which spelled out the sound of the word, and these were followed by a determinative image which specified what sort of person, thing, or activity was meant. Chinese is all pictures, with at most a single secondary image worked in as a visual pun to suggest the sound. Chinese thinks in pictures, and thinking in images and symbols is the very essence of sorcery.

Chinese characters paint the landscape of ancient, mythological China, from the time of the Three Sovereigns, the third millennium BC. They were invented by Foo Shee, the first man, or nearly man, for he and his wife Noo Wa were actually snakes with human faces. (The Hebrew first man, Adam, is similarly credited with the invention of human language, and the serpent at the tree of knowledge suggests a similar constellation of concepts). Foo Shee invented not language but writing, and with the power of the characters he created humanity out of clay.

The characters represent a complete, though admittedly neolithic, landscape, one dominated by female figures, plant life, flood-water, and heavenly signs, a realm of livestock, seeds, fetuses and food. You begin by reciting one of the portal texts, of which the greatest is the first chapter of the Tao Te Ching, visualizing the characters as you speak them. Presently they take on their own life, animate into independence, like the last ideas that pass through your mind as you begin to dream. The diet, meditations and breathing yoga are all aimed at giving you control over this transitional moment so you can enter a state of lucid dreaming.

Whenever I chant the line from that first tremendous chapter of the Tao, "thereby you see its wondrous subtle mysteries," the word for see, gwan, drawn as a bird of prey with claws extended, lifts me out of my physical body, like a soaring hawk, and my eyes take on the telescopic penetration and clarity of a raptor. The word for "wondrous subtlety" miao, is a schematic angular female figure. Beside are marks that mean something small subdivided, that is, the unimaginably small. The symbol for something small is a visual pun on the sign for fetus, which was in the days before ultrasound, the ultimate emblem of the minute and mysterious. Between words gwan and miao my sight takes in not only the tiny and remote, but the hidden, the latent, the implied. The dream scroll from which I read the memorized text becomes a landscape painting, and that becomes animated. The calligraphed characters of the accompanying poem flow into the animated art which is now the actual. In this world, the word and the image and the real precisely coincide, spells are efficacious and magic is a fact.

There is more. All the Chinese characters are built from 214 radicals, beginning with single, simple horizontal line which can represent the horizon, a barrier, heaven, earth or the number one. The last radical is composed of seventeen lines and represents a bamboo syrinx or panpipe, with all its openings and bindings. Between the simplest and the most complex these radicals build not only a world: they also form the microcosm that is the body. It is not by coincidence that there are 213 bones in the human body (including those of the inner ear), and this is roughly the number of components in a complete set of renaissance armor, when it had become a full human exoskeleton. To perform the visualization described above, one must first create for oneself a body of writing, one must internalize the Chinese language, master its classics, and in effect, become a poet, or perhaps one should say, a poem.

A.'s Narrative

I was gradually induced to take over certain menial household duties for Madame Wang, though by then I esteemed them as a privilege.

A woman's home is, like her clothes, not only an expression but an extension of herself, I tended Madame Wang's rooms with the same adoration I directed to her. It was the temple of her presence.

I was in effect her priest, and priesthood requires special vestments. I gradually came to dress in feminine clothing. I accepted this as part of my initiation into shwon pin, the "dark feminine," and soon took pride in being able to dress myself attractively and apply makeup well.

Though elsewhere I dressed in "civilian" clothes, I found myself playing sly games of self-exposure in normal society: betraying in my conversation an undue knowledge of women's artifices.

Also, though I dressed in male attire, I would sometimes wear one ring too many, or a perfume that fell a little too far on the feminine end of the spectrum. I socialized more with women at my workplace, exulting in the fact they felt so comfortable around me, and wondered (with unexpected satisfaction) if the women realized why that was so.

All this describes only the surface. The occult dimension of my relationship will supply the motivation, if not the logic, of these transgender exercises.

Madame Wang was my guide into the spirit realm, my Beatrice, if you will. And though I myself lacked her power to ascend through heavens or plunge into ghost worlds, she could take me with her when she took me by the hand. The first time she did so, it was in her parlor, by the dollhouse. As instructed, I was staring at this, while the incense smoked on the coffee table and she conjured in Chinese, one hand grasping mine. I noticed for the first time that the dollhouse bore a surprising resemblance to the room in which we sat. The furnishings, the curios, all were there, to the finest detail. I remember thinking how odd it was that I had never noticed this before. I tried to decide just what it was in this flawless reproduction that made it seem unreal, that betrayed the fact that these were merely toys. Was it the presence of the three dolls? Examining more carefully the dollhouse furnishings I found that the sense of something askew remained. Perhaps it was that the objects were ever so slightly off-scale? But no, as I looked at them more closely, the proportions proved to be correct. I studied the tiny furnishings, not realizing that I could not have seen them so well from where I sat on the couch, nor could I have picked them up and held them as now I did.

I was inside the doll house room, and the three porcelain figures, were now as real to me as the furniture. The room in which we were now seemed closed and complete, with four walls surrounding the reality within. The four of us now sat at the table and one of the now real female figures poured tea for us all. We sipped and conversed with that wonderful seriousness which you find only in children playing make-believe. We were like four little girls having a dolls' tea party with their dolls—except we were ourselves the dolls. We pretended to be very adult, as only little girls can, and complained of how everything had been better when we were young, of the high price of tea and how difficult money had become—as though we really were grown up ladies. It was childhood regained, life as we find it in a sentimental poem, like Rimbaud's youthful "The Orphans' New Year's Gift" or Heine's "My Child, When We Were Children . . . " It was the more than mortal happiness one glimpses in antique Christmas cards, which one tastes in fruit-shaped Christmas marzipan.

I never mentioned this or my succeeding excursions into the doll house to Doctor Coppelius. He would never have believed they actually took place, and I didn't wish to listen to him grapple with my special and secret reality, leaving the dirty fingerprints of his secular and scientific reality on the perfect, private, and, yes, the holy inner world which had admitted me. And, I confess it, I was afraid he might somehow break the spell. I hadn't anticipated this when I began my treatment, and would not have even begun it had I known the new course my life would abruptly take. Where I did hope he might be of use to me was in coping with the ways in which my new reality devalued the old, made the everyday world seem artificial, implausible, and subtly disproportioned.

$$\oplus\!\!\in$$

Dr. Coppelius's Comment

It was fortunate for science, though sadly of little use to A., that he was in analytic treatment, and here, as his pathology developed. Vienna is the original homeland of psychoanalysis, and if New York has displaced it as the capital, so to speak, the Americans have considerably adulterated Freud's teaching over the last century. Across the Atlantic, medication, personal advice, and popular wisdom have gained favor at the expense of the real work of psychoanalysis. The same propensity to fads and enthusiasms which made America open its doors to Freud has kept them wide for less respectable therapies.

Because I am a traditional analyst, there was no question of my urging A. to break off the relationship with Madame Wang. The work of psychotherapy is to bring the patient to his own realizations: attempts to hasten self-discovery bring treatment to an abrupt end. That is the first lesson the beginning analyst learns.

As the affair with Madame Wang progressed, A. complained of a sense of unreality in his waking life, and the complete cessation of dreams. This was of course impossible: it was A.'s resistance to the content of his dreams, which prevented him from bringing them to conscious awareness.

His wish to reveal his shifting gender, to be exposed, was unexpected. It would have been the suppression of his drives into the unconscious that made his dreams inaccessible to recollection. Such an interior law of secrecy should have resulted in delusions of being watched, paranoia. Not this quasi-exhibitionism!

It is no doubt relevant here that Madame Wang would catechize him regarding his lowly, servile and feminized state, requiring him to to admit aloud, that he was her property, a neutered object, a thing, a feminine plaything, a doll. The acknowledgment of A.'s emerging feminine identity, which Madame Wang required of him, and which he obliquely asked of others, finally pointed to a problem less sexual than existential.

A plausible, rational (and for those very reasons inadequate when we are examining the unconscious!) explanation might be that, A., coming awkwardly to terms with a non-binary gender identity, was starved for any validation, positive or negative.

But we might more usefully wonder whether the archaic and impractical education A. received, and the way he had shaped his character, finding his models in the obscure barbarities of late Latin literature, hadn't, from the outset, compromised his reality? One might plausibly take the point of view that A.'s was an ontological problem, one that should be understood in occult rather than psychological terms. I realize this diagnosis falls outside the accepted categories of psychology, but I implore the reader to form his judgment on the facts when they are fully presented.

Was A. now crossing gender boundaries because he had already crossed metaphysical ones? This explanation alone seems adequate to account for his desperate need to be reassured of his being. For the impression I received in our analytic hours was that, as much as A. longed to be told what he was, directly by Madame Wang, and indirectly by his female co-workers, he longed even more ardently to be reassured that he was.

A.'s narcissistic predicament, hypnotized by his feminine image in the mirror, may have less to do with vanity or homosexual tendencies, than with the need to find irrefutable evidence of his existence.

If it were a true psychosis developing, I would have expected delusions. When the ego falters, the repressed emerges into waking beliefs as it does in dreams. But this was not the situation. His sorcerer's apprenticeship to Madame Wang was assuredly unwholesome, but it was by no means a delusion. A. was not in flight from reality, though his reality was now so exotic as to almost constitute an alternate world.

33

A.'s Narrative

At times I could now hear far distant conversations, though not clearly enough to get more than the general drift. I began to foresee events, though only a few seconds in the future. I saw the water-glass tip before the man at the next table in the restaurant knocked it over reaching for the bread-basket. I would have thought I was losing my mind if these telepathic and precognitive events had had any significance, even a purely personal one. But they were random and trivial. Madame Wang explained to me that these new awarenesses were signs of spiritual progress.

I advanced in the spiritual disciple—I use the term discipline advisedly. Initiation comes at a painful price. The figurative death of the self must be physically furthered and confirmed. Madame Wang liked to make this point with a rather wicked quotation from Confucius, the famous line from the fourth book of the Analects,

The superior man cherishes punishment; the paltry person wants to be coddled.

Of course it's rather better in the Chinese, where the world for punishment, shing, sounds like a riding crop swishing briskly through the air.

And this was in fact a primary means by which Madame Wang hastened my progress to, as she put it, "a gallop." Afterwards she would stand me in front of a mirror so I could see my mouth open in an involuntary astonished "O," my foundation-whitened cheeks striped with mascara-blackened tears, the very picture of punishment. Mine were the fantastic sorrows of a weeping Pierrot, whose pale face betrays his ghostly status. At such times I felt a spiritual thrill as Madame Wang addressed me as "sweety," with her special malicious grin. Gender was just another surpassable limit of the mortal condition.

Under her maternal command, beneath her punishing hand, I attained a sense of helpless wonder, like the awe an infant feels before his (to him) godlike parents. As the great twenty-eighth chapter of the Dao De Jing says,

the eternal power of the Dao never leaves him,
and he returns, comes home to a childlike state

Doctor Coppelius's Comment

Madame Wang was transforming A. in ways for which the psychiatric case histories afforded me no precedent. The closest parallels I could arrive at were in the Asian tales of ghosts and fox-spirits who become romantically involved with living men, and drain them of their chee, their vital force. They carry out these parasitic liaisons for the endless extension of their own life spans, or to restore their energies exhausted by acts of sorcery. I had viewed this analogy, albeit with a shudder, as a psychological clue, rather than an investigative fact.

Another oddity which I dismissed at the time as an irrelevant impression, but which I am now inclined to take rather more seriously, is the change in A.'s physical appearance. When he first came to me he was a presentable, neatly dressed man, with shoes always shined, never in need of a shave or slovenly in any detail. As time went on his complexion became more pale and even, the faint blotches and blemishes which one finds on any adult male's face were no longer visible. I assumed he taken to wearing foundation and makeup. He kept this indulgence within acceptable limits, though he finally arrived at a complexion which was a little unnaturally natural, a shade too smooth, like that of a computer generated character. His skin had taken on the translucence of—I cannot withhold an accurate detail of clinical observation merely because it may make a melodramatic impression—of fine porcelain. With the advantage of hindsight, I now see that I should have insisted on a physical examination. I considered doing so, but resisted this out of a sense of scientific delicacy. An illness of suspected psychosomatic origin would justify such a proceeding, but a psychosomatic cosmetic effect? That would be an inquiry for a beautician, not a physician!

Shortly before A. ceased his treatment, I had a dream of him, in which he appeared with one of his eyes heavily masacara'd, like the character Alex in the film Clockwork Orange. The name connection, A. becoming Alex, is easily understood, but the reference to Kubrick's film, and the Burgess novel on which it is based, is more revealing.

The title comes from a Cockney saying, "Queer as a clockwork orange." Burgess used the phrase to describe Alex's mental reconditioning, which was meant to make of him a docile automaton, a human robot programmed to social norms. The phrase "clockwork orange" implies a replacement of the organic by the mechanical, or an impossible fusion of the nature and art.

Though an analyst's dreams are ordinarily irrelevant clinically, in this particular case, where the facts were so far from ordinary, I should perhaps have taken it as a clue which might be fruitfully pursued.

Perhaps Madame Wang's regimen was merely behavior modification, brainwashing, with an overlay of exotic and erotic elements. But this explanation leaves a number of questions unanswered.

A. never complained of anxiety, but rather of a mounting sense of unreality. Along with this there was the apparent but impossible disappearance of his dreams. Dreams are the lifeblood of the psyche—the very definition of artificial intelligence is an intelligence which cannot dream. Very well, you may say, the dreams were repressed. But repression without anxiety? Another oddity was the complete absence of Fehlleistungen, *verbal misfires, what they call in English*

"Freudian Slips," which always betray the unconscious. It was as though A. no longer had an unconscious.

It seemed as though A.'s sense of unreality was well founded. From the new texturelessness of his skin to the apparent vanishing of his unconscious, he seemed to undergoing a gradual idealization, becoming an abstracted representation of person, a figure to be added to Madame Wang's wunderkammer, a further Frozen Charlotte to stand in the series with her sister figurines.

I cannot help but wonder how matters turned out for him. In any event, the following is the final record of our sessions.

ā́ā́ā́

A.'s Narrative

To be a toy, to be a doll—this turned out to be my final fantasy. To stand before the mirror that shows my painted face, to approach it as closely as I do when applying eye-shadow, and never fog the glass with living breath!

Dolls themselves go back as far as human artifacts and, technically, one could include in their number small statues of deities, medical models, even action figures, but the preponderance of dolls represent adult females and are intended to be played with by girls. Barbie *is the best known contemporary example, and may be taken as paradigmatic. For a little girl,* Barbie *is a model of imagined future femininity. She is dressed, coiffed, and admired by her young owner—and at times used to act out anxieties regarding the vaguely understood facts of life.* Barbies *are outgrown at the very point when a girl becomes a young woman and herself takes on the feminine traits* Barbie *only suggests.*

For me a doll represents something similar yet significantly different. Yes, a doll is a paradigm of femininity, but a femininity that can never be literally realized. A doll's stylized, exaggerated proportions and especially the graphic idealizing of the face—circles of rouge on the cheeks, intensely red pouting lips on a porcelain-perfect face, long lashes on over-sized eyes—this was the ideal for which I strove in my own application of makeup. To create a face that was less an image than an icon, more a graphic symbol than a physical reality.

For me the most important aspect of a doll is one that is not shown and indeed is not there to be seen: its genderlessness, the flat dead level of plastic in place of a vulva was like a poignant reflection my own indefiniteness—what Madame Wang characterized as my identification with the limitless.

— 144 —

There is more. I want to be a doll—so as to be dressed, played with, and owned by a girl.

I have no aspiration towards womanhood, the tender bonds of maternity, nor to femaleness and the biological fine detail of fecundity, nor am I ambitious for femininity, which includes the subtly competitive social world of girls, in which generosity and fairness are not always foremost:

Rather, I envision an idyll of girlish pastimes and play, a looking-glass world into which I can bluff my way by a program of spectral resemblances. I am a ghost attempting to haunt a dollhouse.

Madame Wang's Journal

I have always loved miniatures, charm bracelets, tiny vignettes and things that fit in lockets.

I breathe a sigh of satisfaction as I add the fourth figure to my doll collection. These creatures are so happy when the process is completed. You tell by the sly little smiles on their rosebud lips and between the large red rouge circles on their round and shining cheeks. There are those who court immortality in vampiric wise, draining males of their yang energy until they sicken and waste away. Cruel and lewd, it seems to me, this draining a man of life through the loins. I prefer submissive, feminine men, whom I lighten of their masculine force in exquisite anticipations of pleasure, the interminable sweetness of deferred release. I deprive them of their virility along with their actuality, I domesticate the male. I fix him, to use the coy little euphemism current among pet owners, but leave him a blissful if diminished existence. Out in the wild, the world of men, these aggression-impaired boys would hardly fare so well. They're far better off with me, in my wunderkammer of implausible desires, my miniature circus of polite behavior, my microcosmic finishing school and theatre of charm.

⚬⚬
⚬

So we sit together, frozen, the penultimate bell all tolled, and you watch the doll, still and silent as the music fades away. "Stand up," I say—an invitation, not a command. You rise to your feet, unsteady after sitting for so long (or has it been long at all, you wonder idly). I walk towards you, once again fingering my honey gold crystal, and we stand before each other, stand before Judgement, our dance weighed against itself before the eyes of Maat.

"You may, if you wish," I say. "If not, you are dismissed. The last tale can not be told, as if by a teacher to a pupil. It must be shared." You take me in, this begotten moonchild-sunbastard hybrid, this homunculus of paper and mirage in the shape of a person. You take in the hair that falls in tangles, the skin that defies neat descriptors, the painted lips chapped from their service and the eyes that look far too old for the face that contains them—and then your fingers are in that hair, your arms are wrapped around my shoulders, and I take the kiss, gentle as a nightingale on my lips even as our bodies press together.

We do not know one another, but are not strangers, especially not now, as our breath mingles with the other's and our limbs lock us together. Your hands skitter up and down my body like spiders, exploring, touching, eager and shaky, and I feel your fear, and I nip at your neck gently, kissing up the side of your cheek to your earlobe, where, as the clothes begin to come off, as this final stage of the operation begins, I start to whisper, even as your fingers begin to creep down my stomach and to slip beneath silk:

"What have we learned?" I ask. "What knowledge have we gained from this dialectic? What horrors lie out there still? What eeriness awaits in this final tale, as we watch, voyeurs, as…"

DR. FRANKENSTEIN DABBLES IN SELF-DISCOVERY

C. C. Rayne

The fingers don't fit. No gloves to be found. I cut them carefully, snip off the parts that have molded, sterilize the dead flesh with a hot iron.

But when I try to sew them onto myself, *into* myself, with my one remaining hand, the work doesn't take. The surgical thread breaks. Thin threads of flesh fall wetly down onto the floorboards.

Outside the cottage, there's a muted rumble of thunder. A wave crashes violently on the rocky shore.

With a sigh, I let myself collapse down into the velvet armchair in the corner of the cottage. Across the room, the covered mirror looms over me. I slouch and glare at my unfinished work, as if that will make it better. Or make me feel better.

It does neither, of course.

Science is a nine-out-of-ten business. That's something that I learned at Ingolstadt. They never actually gave me my medical degree, but I've come to care less about that part than I used to.

On the good, predictable, legal side of science, nine-out-of-ten refers to the procedures and creations that go right. Before a station failure, most train rides will be smooth. An appendectomy will go harmlessly, almost every time.

My side of science isn't predictable, and most others see it as abomination. It isn't illegal, but only because no one can conceive of its horrors long enough to pass a law. For me, nine out of ten is about failures. Attempt after attempt that is guaranteed to rip, ruin, blow up, burn out, break down.

Yet here I am—in a one-room cottage on a rainswept island, sitting amidst an unsuccessful butchery, old sweat soaked through my shirt, one hand missing all its digits, and my garters stained with other people's blood.

I push myself out of the chair, and run the gory, ground-up hand through my hair. I've hit this fit of pique a dozen times before. I know that the only balm to make it blow over is work. Always, always, focus on the work.

Mutilation and creation are essentially the same thing. You need more than one attempt to get them right.

✠

Henry is my assistant today. All too cheerful and all too willing. He leans against the graveyard fence and pretends at nonchalance while I dig up dirt and desacralize the grave of someone's recently-deceased father.

When he starts to whistle a tune, I am forced to pause my work and glare at him. He feels the force of my narrowed brow from underneath the black-brimmed hat. He wilts, like a sweet plant in the scorching sun.

"Sorry, sorry, I'm sorry," he spills out. "Too much attention. I'm just nervous, though."

"Don't be."

I turn away and devote myself to digging.

Footsteps, careful on the hallowed grass, alert me that he's abandoned the fence post and come to watch. Another glare wouldn't help my case, so I permit it. He sits at the side of the grave I've dug up, tapping a tarantelle on his thigh. His eyes jitter and jump in his skull like fleeing fish.

"Henry, why are you nervous?" I ask him.

The casket is uncovered, and I've unclasped the lid. There's not enough space to open it up fully. I've been reduced to rooting around in a couple feet of darkness with one hand outstretched. The other hand – the stump-one, missing its fingers - holds the casket lid aloft.

"Someone could come, and…I don't know. It makes me very worried, Victor. Something could…*happen*."

"Exactly," I say.

Beneath my grasping hand: something soft and wet. Human flesh, hard in strange places. Dead but not yet decaying. Probably the leg, or perhaps the hip. But I know what I came here looking for.

This man was hanged in town two days ago for the crime of murder. I watched the hanging. I sketched from a restaurant balcony, and even now, there's a piece of paper in my pocket that shows him a moment before his neck snapped. He was wild-eyed, blonde hair and beautiful cheekbones. The curve of his shoulder struck me as particularly gorgeous.

I envy gorgeous things. I always have. Perhaps I'm spoiled. I grew up well, and yet I still want more.

But then again: if I'm smart enough to see something, I should take it. Take it and break it and make it all mine.

I've been reinventing my body all my life. This is simply the next step in the process.

My hand slides upwards. Palm over clammy skin, giving way to rough rib, and then finally: tough gristle muscle and solid bone.

I switch positions. There's a knife in my glove. Even with damaged fingers, I am an expert wielder. I dig the blade in and slice wide, carving through the layers down to the meat. Something squirts. Henry makes a noise like he's going to be sick.

The part of me that loves him is sorry to give him grief. But the bigger part of me is wild-happy with achievement. I laugh, half at him, as I drag the whole limb free.

"Something could always happen," I say. "I *want* it to happen. It's the only way to live."

E

It would make the most sense for me to leave attempts on the whole limb until after a resounding success with the hand and fingers.

Patience, Professor Krempe would have said to me in my surgical labs, years ago. *Patience is what makes a great man great.*

I will most certainly be great. I have not always been a man, though. And furthermore, I have *never* been a patient man.

So off comes the remainder of my right arm. Clean and simple.

There's something perverse in this choice of mutilation. I am right-handed, like the vast majority are. But no. I have something to prove. A stretch towards perfection: I will accomplish my goals using my weak side, or not at all. I will cut off all avenues of anything other than ambition.

And thus, I cut off my arm.

I've sent Henry away for the day, and I have not called Elizabeth, so it's just me in the cottage. My curved knife is heated, and the rag goes between my teeth. I bite down. The blade goes in.

Enamel still shatters, from the sonic force of the scream. Outside, something howls horribly, and the shack trembles. Another storm? Or the wail of a fog horn, warning the town away?

Good. They should stay far away from me. That's how I like it.

There is a barrier in the mind, a tall grey wall that we erect to stop ourselves from doing personal damage. It's there for a reason, and I do not begrudge it. I have learned to circumvent it for my self-surgeries.

My circumvention does not lessen the pain, though. Nor does it increase my ability to bear it.

As I lie and twitch in my own blood, my severed right arm at a jarring angle in the peripheral of my vision, I let the waves wash over me. I come once again to the grim understanding that this is a necessary evil. Harm first, and healing second.

Eventually, the agony subsides to a horrible roar. I grimace and drag myself up to my surgical table. I find the cold dead arm and shoulder of the hanged man, freshly prepped and washed in salt water. I've plugged wires into it for the electrification. They dangle sharply from the limb's white bulkiness like limp, loose veins.

Even with all the changes, I am still struck with that same memory. The gorgeous curve of arm and shoulder, fresh in my brain, sparking envy and desire as I watched the man swing.

Beside me, Henry buried his face in my chest, distraught. I had shared no such symptoms.

I want to look like that, I had thought to myself hungrily.

Only one way to make it happen.

I only have one working hand with which to sew. I trap the haunch of shoulder between the table and the bleeding stump. I set to work. Stitch, stitch, stitch. Flares of pain where the needle pricks my living skin. Dull nothing when it pricks the other man's.

Perhaps ten minutes elapse. It could have been a century. I do not care. All I know is that somehow, I graft the shoulder onto myself slowly, a hand hanging limply at the end of it. I stagger to my feet, shoes slick on the pool of my own blood.

I finally throw the switch.

Lightning sparks down from the weathervane. It trickles light-fast through the wires I embedded in the ceiling. It crackles through the long wires and the dead cells, and buries itself in my bones.

When I come to consciousness an hour later, my shoulder is new, living, fresh-flesh that curves sinuously under my palm. I run a hand along it and feel triumph pool deep in my belly.

For the first time since I arrived in the cottage, I gather the courage to look into the mirror. I stand off to the side, unwilling to see my as-yet-unchanged face, but longing to see the new parts of my body.

The shoulder fits. The angle is just as gorgeous as it was on the dead man. More so, on me.

I think idly about the *crack* that his neck made, trying to see if I feel anything sad or sympathetic. But the pulse of dark joy in my stomach quickly drowns it out.

In the mirror, I see the side of my face, only a sliver. The old mouth quirks up in a cold smile. The new hand picks up a well-worn butcher's knife.

☿

Elizabeth is my assistant today. She's long since grown tired of my tricks. But she still loves me, just like Henry loves me, drawn in by the magnetic field of a man who can't stop wanting more.

The two of them trailed after me to this island, forlorn and love-sick, and I let them. That's probably monstrous of me. I don't really care. I need the help to finish what I've started.

Creating life anew. Once, I dreamed of making a unique man, one stitched together from the limbs and lives of corpses and brought to life in front of me. I've given up on that dream. It's still viable. The science all checks out.

But why make a second man when I could remake myself?

Why give the spark of selfhood to someone else?

Who deserves a new form more than me?

Elizabeth stands still at the gate of the graveyard. Her dress rustles in the wind. Autumn leaves blow through the hem, dancing in time with her clothing, but she stays stoic, a marble statue of a woman.

Behind her, I sit cross-legged on a nearby crypt, my hands in my jacket pocket, my curls whipping wild around my head.

I contemplate the barren options I possess.

To resew myself, I need bodies that are at least somewhat recently dead. The island affords me privacy, but that comes at the cost of a lack of charnel-houses. Executions do occur, but they are few and far between. And I want to continue my work. It feels right. It's the only thing that does.

What to do?

From behind me, a sigh.

"Are you nervous?" I ask.

"No," Elizabeth says. "I'm…concerned."

I can't really fault her for that, but I do nonetheless.

"By me, or by my work?"

"Does it matter?" she says. Her frame is faintly trembling, her skin prickled up with goosebumps in the cold breeze, her muscles tense. "Aren't you one with your work by this point, anyway?"

Her eyes are fixed firmly on my new shoulder. It's distinguishable, even under my cloak and overcoat. I favor the old, outdated side now. The new part of my body is lighter, lither, stronger.

As she stares at it, gaze boring through fabric and filament, I could swear I feel the dead man's fingers twitch of their own accord.

Oddly enough, the sensation does not displease me.

Instead, it sparks a new thought in my mind, one that writhes around like captive lightning.

"I'm doing my best," I say, and smile at her. "Why don't you go back to the inn, Elizabeth? Get an early night."

"If that's what you wish, Victor."

She stalks away. Her footsteps leave gravel and grimness in their wake.

She's known me too long. We grew up girls together, after all. Then, once I changed, the world was suddenly ready to see us as a perfect pair.

I couldn't tell you truly if I love her. There's no way to tell if you love the people you're born beside, really. It's expected of you so long that it becomes not a feeling, but a habit.

Still. Old habits die hard.

And I know how I'm going to get the next piece of myself.

I skulk around the seedy parts of town later that afternoon. There's a tall, reedy fisherman by the docks. He bears the brand of a convicted thief, destined for the gallows on a single repeat offense. He sits on the pier and weaves fishnets, fixes sails, his gaze intent on the folds of fabric that lie on his leg.

His leg. Yes.

I quite like his leg.

I stare from the shadows for a while at the curve of his calf. The length of his muscle. The strong flesh, the fine ankle, the working knee.

It's beautiful. It's beautiful. And I want it, stitched to my skin, sawed bone meeting sawed bone. I want it to be a part of me.

I want it to *be* me.

It is the work of a mere few moments to talk my way into the bailiff's house and snatch a gold cup when his back is turned. Late that night, I plant the cup amongst the fisherman's nets once he has left the dock. It gleams in the moonlight, the metal icy cold.

The hunt and search and trial take a few days more than I would like. But the end of the week brings me my wish. The fisherman, neck new-broken on the gallows, is buried in the graveyard.

He's only a few feet down.

It's far too easy to dig.

When I chop my left leg off, the pain sends my vision shimmering white, but I hold on. I hold on through the ripping and the sewing, through the times where my consciousness fades out as blood loss and fatigue take their toll.

But I always get back up again. Envy and eagerness and electricity babble ceaselessly back and forth in my brain.

And when I finally flip the switch—

∇

Elizabeth and Henry see me about town the next day, and they know. Of course they know. My friends and lovers, they have known from the beginning.

But even if they wanted to say something, who would they tell? Who would believe them?

I walk with a confidence and strength I have not had since childhood. My new foot is too hale and hearty for its boot, and almost wears the sole to shreds on the cobblestone. When I put my hand to the stitched skin, I can feel its firmness and ripeness. I can almost sense the sparks of life buzzing within.

The fisherman's leg takes me down streets I do not know. It makes me wander and detour, sends me to the schools and the piers, to strange stores and unfamiliar places of worship. A world of knowledge, burnt into my new nerves.

Science is sweat and tears, blood and guts, weal and woe. Many people turn away from it because of this. They fail to see that it's the dearest form of truth. They fail to see that what scientists do is ultimate bravery.

We stare life in the face.

I have always known in my bones that I would die before I'd lose control of my own body. And here and now, despite the changes, I feel more autonomy, more control, than I think I ever have.

Because for all the newness and irregularity, these changes were my own, wrought by my own hand. This was all a choice, made by none other than me.

⚲

I am trapped in the cottage one evening by a wild wind and a lightning storm. Abovehead, there is an irregular *crack* whenever the rod I installed gathers another bolt of energy. Outside, angry foam splatters on the rocks. This place was built on a precipice. It was designed to fall.

Yet here it stands. Alone and solitary, but alive.

Just like me.

I slouch alone all night in the velvet armchair and stare at the slick metal tables, the buckets and piles of unused parts, the gore that clogs the bathroom drain. My eyes are narrowed, crusted with sweat. A knife dangles in my brand new fingers. Waiting. Waiting.

I could have asked Henry to join me tonight. Or Elizabeth. Or both. Innocent company - or less innocent, perhaps. There would have been no shame in that.

But I've seen the way they look at me, now that I've changed.

Did they always look at me that way? When did it start? Was it the body-snatching and limb-sewing?

Or was it before? Did it start further back than then?

Was it when I changed the first time round? When I stopped being the old me, and started being myself?

I flick my new wrist. My *better* wrist.

The surgical knife flies forward into the mirror.

The sound of glass breaking doesn't even register. Instead, I watch as my reflection goes from smooth to jagged, a single piece broken freshly into many fragments. The fault lines carve channels through my face. That face I have so often tried to avoid.

Crunched down in the chair, I feel the cottage rock with the force of the world's great storm. Everything from everyone, wrapped up in clouds and crushing force, bears down to bury me whole.

I don't bother to do anything about it. That part is out of my control.

Instead, I stare at my cracked face.

It is comfortable to look at, for the very first time.

An idea blooms, like a plant, or a tumor, or some strange and cancerous growth. It spreads itself in a web throughout me, until I finally move of my own accord.

When I stumble out into the storm, the force of the gale nearly whips me off the precipice, down to the rocks below.

I can picture it happening in my mind. The body of Victor Frankenstein could be broken uncontrollably into pieces, the stitches separated by sharp stone. My separate segments would washed away from one another, my new arm still grasping for the rest of me.

Instead, I grit my teeth and pull my coat tighter around my body, my hat down further over my brow. I stumble forward, towards the quiet village. Everyone will be in their homes by now. No one cares to be out in this overwhelming storm.

No one will be even slightly prepared for me.

In my pocket, my knife lies ready beside needle and thread. In my arm-veins and leg-muscles, the two dead men make me stagger. It's almost as if they know what I plan to do.

But no matter what strange route they force me to take, I pull myself back on track.

No more nine out of ten. No room for error.

There's only room for me.

⚷

There is a version where I am caught immediately. The mad doctor is stopped before he could slaughter the town.

There is another version: I get a few people, but someone fights back. Same outcome, with a little more blood and gore.

It's a large village, honestly. The odds that I could murder in my own name and get away with it are astronomically low.

But then again, there are many versions, and there will always be more. The version where I was first born a man, and never changed at all. The version where I made a creature, instead of making me. The version where I learned to love it, and did not turn away.

What use are those versions?

This is my version now. I'll sew together the parts that I desire. All the rest, they'll live in the scrap bucket.

They're nothing but dead meat.

Henry and Elizabeth find me the next morning, as the sun rises over the becalmed sea. They pick their way down through the bodies that bleed faintly on the steps of the small inn. They make it through the streets, where flotsam and jetsam mix with ravenous seagulls that feast on the townsfolk's remains.

They find me sitting on the shoreline below. I still wear my coat, but my hat is gone, and my new hair flows free in the wind. I am perched on one of the rocks that might well have dashed me to pieces in a careless fall.

I am whole now, however.

I always will be - though I never will be again.

Henry looks at my face with horror. Elizabeth, with concern. I blink back at them through two new eyes. The grey one, I gathered from a young bartender. The green one was first from the town bailiff, or maybe from his daughter.

When I smile, I feel stitches split around my mouth. Thousands of pieces of carefully-selected skin have not yet fully healed. My seams rip at the edges, and streams of blood go dripping down my jaw.

"Something's happened," I say to them. "I got it right."

POSTLUDE:
HEAVENLY SHADES OF NIGHT ARE FALLING

The dance breaks, and we roll off of each other, and we lay there on the bed, looking up at the canopy hanging above us, rose madder with a smattering of silver stars.

What happened between us is between us, and our bodies are once again as independent as flesh can ever really pretend to be, and I turn and look you in the eyes, reaching up to stroke your cheek.

"How are you feeling?" I ask.

You search for the words, trying to fit the emotions into the shackled shape of words, before you realize that it was a trick question. "With my heart. With my mind. With…"

"Everything," I finish, and you nod. "You can stay the night if you wish, but I have to hit the road by seven." I stretch and throw my legs over the edge of the mattress, slipping into a flowing black robe, and toss you a t-shirt. It's a size too big, hand-printed: apathy feeds the machine, it reads, and you pull it on, joining me on the carpet.

"Come on out," I say, opening the door, stepping out into the cricket-scored air, brandishing a joint that seemed to appear from thin air. You follow, and you sit on the step while I stand and light the tip.

We look up at the sky, at the moon that's waning again, at the clouds of light pollution hiding the dreaming stars. Our breath joins the chirping nightbirds, the softly singing insects, the burble of a creek somewhere in the woods nearby. Everything feels sharp and colorful and real, even as the night air turns everything grayscale.

"Thank you," I say, softly, puffing lightly on the thyme-tinted smoke. "For listening."

You take the j, considering the spiraling smoke, watching it die, watching it just become part of the atmosphere. We stand there, bound and unbound all at once, torn asunder and holy and whole and half-blooded and half-dead, changing and dying and breathing and living and doing it all again and again and again.

The firepit glows a ruddy orange, only coal and ash and memory left behind.

We stand, watching deep pink ribbons snake through the cloudy night sky, tasting candy corn in the back of our throats even through the smoke, and the World turns and turns and turns on its string, all of us tangled up in her pendulum swing, riding the synchronicity highway straight to hell.

Somewhere in the woods, beneath a sliver of yearning moon, a coyote howls and pulls the sky down on top of us, draping us in tender darkness as we pass our torch and the smoke curls out of our lips, spiraling up to heaven.

something strange happened last night
deep in the graveyard, a glow was thrown
upon the overbrush
and I felt like *something* saw me

Now I'm scraping past the way I came

CONTRIBUTOR BIOS

Lennox Rex ("Birthday Suit") is an Oregonian raised in Southern California, Lennox Rex has always been enamored with storytelling. His work also appears in *HorrorScope Volume 3*, *Doors of Darkness*, and the Halloween 2023 issue of *The Sirens Call eZine*. To him, life is best enjoyed with music, body mods, and plenty of coffee and sweets. He lives with his husband, their three children, possibly too many pets, and nowhere near enough books.

Thea Maeve ("Fresh Meat", she/fae) is a horror and dark fantasy writer living in Phoenix. Her works often draw from her own perspectives as a trans woman, infusing visceral storytelling and queer concepts into her works. She has works published in *Cosmic Horror Monthly*, *Howls From Hell*, and *Howls From the Wreckage*. She can be occasionally found streaming horror games like Stardew Valley, and cozy indie games like Outlast on Twitch @SpookyMaevey. She also is a captain and coach of ALPHA ice hockey, which is the LGBTQ+ ice hockey league in Arizona, where she teaches new skaters how to play the game and find a welcoming queer community in the sport.)

Alicia Hilton ("Death Taught Me How to Live") is an author, editor, arbitrator, professor, and former FBI Special Agent. She believes in angels and demons, magic, and monsters. Her work has appeared in *Akashic Books*, *Creepy Podcast*, *Daily Science Fiction*, *Litro*, *Mslexia*, *Neon*, *Space & Time*, *Unnerving*, *Vastarien*, *Year's Best Hardcore Horror Volumes 4, 5 & 6*, and elsewhere. She is a member of the Horror Writers Association, the Science Fiction and Fantasy Poetry Association, and the Science Fiction and Fantasy Writers Association. Her website is https://aliciahilton.com. Follow her on Twitter @aliciahilton01 and Bluesky aliciahilton.bsky.social.

Ju Collins ("Seen", they/them) is a nonbinary person who grew up and currently resides in Newfoundland and Labrador. They are

inspired to write stories about lgbtqia2S+ folks in ways that feel genuine and relatable in order
to normalize the lives (and horrors) of those who live outside the binary world. They live with their partner in rural Newfoundland with their 2 French Bulldogs.

Mave Goren ("The Moss Witch of the Cascade Mountains") is an author, musician, radio host and semi-professional bog witch. A native of Victorian Flatbush, Brooklyn, you can find her haunting your local library. She has also released *Enter the Cyclopean Hall* a chapbook of stories for Bottlecap Press.

Michelle Jacklyn Miller ("Wolformation") Michelle Jacklyn Miller is an international best-selling author of LGBTQIA+ fiction. She is a transgender woman who served in the US Army with 1 deployment to Iraq. She has a BA in Spanish and has published 7 books. She currently lives in Maryland.

Madeleine Varley ("Fly") is a high school junior in Asheville, North Carolina. Along with their highschool work they are taking courses in computer science and Mandarin. They are the middle of three siblings and enjoy reading, running, and playing or watching games like *Dungeons & Dragons*.

E. B. Novetti ("Figs for Thistles") E.B. Novetti is an author and engineer with a specialization in the impact of large language models (LLMs). She holds an M.S. in Computer Science and an M.F.A. in Fiction. Novetti lives in the American West. https://ebnovetti.com/

R.S. Saha ("Bleed for Your Wishes") is a queer Tamil American editor, translator, and writer. They translate Tamil short stories and novels to English. They also write speculative fiction and have been published by Baffling Magazine. When Saha is not writing, they are reading, playing video games, rewatching a show they've seen ten times already, or hanging out with their friends' dogs. They can be found @SahardlyTrying on Twitter.

Mildred Faintly ("Frozen Charlotte") is a transgender woman who writes book reviews for the SF/Fantasy literary magazine *96thofoctober.com*. She earned a doctorate in classics under another name in another life; this rendered her entirely unemployable and for some years not very good company. She finally found work as a high school math teacher, where she explained to parents the dispiriting facts of how numerical grades are averaged. In the classroom, her talents were more meaningfully brought into play deciding who really needed to use the bathroom, and inflating grades (those impromptu lessons in averages never really "took.") Now retired, she is translating the sweetly melancholy poems of Li Qing Zhao, a brilliant and defiant woman of the Sung dynasty, and enjoying the life of a literary recluse in a bamboo grove somewhere in New Jersey. Her translation from Yiddish of the lesbian poet Anna Margolin's poetry is being published by Punctum Books, while her translation of *Styx*, Else Lasker-Schüler's first book of poems, will be published by the Ben Yehuda Press.

C. C. Rayne ("Dr. Frankenstein Dabbles in Self-Discovery") is a writer, actor, and creator based on the East Coast. A lover of all things weird and discontented, C. C.'s work blends the magical with the mundane, and the silly with the strange. You can read more of C. C. 's stories in *The Deeps, The Razor, Sublunary Review, Demons and Death Drops, and Fish Gather To Listen: An Anthology of Underwater Horror*. C. C. 's poetry can be found in such places as *The Dread Machine, Soft Star Magazine, Eye to the Telescope*, and *moth eaten mag*.

Dillon Rae Oliver (epigraph, "untitled") is a non-binary artist hailing from Northeast Ohio. Performing music under the moniker "Skeleton Drive", Dillon has self-released several collections of their special brand of sad indie songs since their start as an artist in 2018. On top of their passion for music, Dillon also enjoys creating digital art, doodling little characters, and writing poetry when certain inspirations hit."

Fritz Dries (editor) is a poet and laborer from Ontario. He has published two collections, Four Seconds and Bury Your Teeth in the Yard.

v.f. thompson (editor) is just compost in training. She can be found clowning around Kalamazoo, MI.

Levi L. is and always shall be. Check out more of their work at 2headedcoralsnake.com.

ACKNOWLEDGEMENTS

This book would not have been possible without the support of readers like you, and we would like to extend a hearty thank you to all of the following fine folks who contributed to this book's fundraiser over on Indiegogo! Those people include…

Charlotte Gremel, Antoinette Del Rae, Tricia Flowers, Alex Riley, jessica gilbert, Makarenna Binimelis, Ju Collins, Lexx Ambrose, Heidi Luby, Heather Green, Carter Cesareo, charlearning, kungfuturtle, Mal Harrigan, Heather Tobin, blaneyma1, Vanessa Hillier, Emily Brent, Dion Power, Alison Power, kpuddister3, Ally Thoden, Kellan McCormick, Leilani Roser, Kirsten Craig, Courtney Bennett, Lisa Campbell, Bridgit Shebib, Emily Shebib, Solaris O'Dell, Christina White, Oma Meade, Soundararajan Varathappan, Mitchell Noel, Kayla Dober, Josh Søn Af Mørten, Stephen Maley, Amanda Hickman, Meagan Thompson, Kel Craghead, Katelyn Hayden, Vivek Subramanian, Nikki Kumar, Karan Kaul, Beth Stephens, Beth Stephens, Dan S, Kat Jepson, Rowan Wright, kale woods, Mathias Lobban, Wendy Boden, Krista Lindemann, Amanda Keith, dasue123, Rebecca Mead, Sy Mander, skandarks, Ria Doolan, Shanmugam Krishnasamy, Sephi Coleman-Tunney, Jay J, Asherah Sussmeine!

… not to mention our very first supporter on Patreon, **Poppet!**

… as well as MV Publishing and Kelly Thompson for partnering with dpl on this project and helping make it a reality.

Enjoy this book? Consider subscribing to future issues
and other Dionysian Public Library projects at
patreon.com/dionysianpubliclibrary.

Don't want to subscribe, but want to be kept in the loop?
Visit us at dionysianpubliclibrary.com or follow us at

Twitter: @DPublicLibrary
Facebook: DioPublicLibrary
Tumblr: dionysianpubliclibrary
Insta: @dionysianpubliclibrary

You can also find our editors, Fritz Dries and v.f. thompson, on Twitter at
@howlingmoth and @VF_Thompson respectively.

Interested in contributing to future projects?
Take a gander at dionysianpubliclibrary.com/submissions